ROGUE RESCUE

ROGUE RESCUE

ROGUE AGENTS OF MAGIC™ BOOK 3

TR CAMERON   MICHAEL ANDERLE   MARTHA CARR

DISRUPTIVE IMAGINATION®

LMBPN Publishing
PMB 196, 2540 South Maryland Pkwy
Las Vegas, NV 89109

Version 1.00, October, 2021
ebook ISBN: 978-1-68500-545-0
Print ISBN: 978-1-68500-546-7

THE ROGUE RESCUE TEAM

Thanks to our JIT Readers:

Thomas Ogden
Wendy L Bonell
Dave Hicks
Zacc Pelter
Dorothy Lloyd

If we've missed anyone, please let us know!

Editor
Skyhunter Editing Team

For those who seek wonder around every corner and in each turning page. And, as always, for Dylan and Laurel.

— *TR Cameron*

CHAPTER ONE

Kevin Serrano paced the room behind the two curved desks occupied by his technicians. Monitors filled the wall in front of them, some mammoth and others only large, their flat screens showing his teams moving into position. The techs operated drones flying high above the scene, their enhanced optics permitting them to remain far enough away that the targets wouldn't hear them. Fortunately, it was a crisp and cloudless night, probably the best environment imaginable for the operation about to take place. *Sometimes, the good guys get lucky.*

Another monitor displayed a broader view of the area in Georgetown where the target brownstone was. The image was a computer rendering overlaid on a drone feed, with small icons representing police presence in motion at various points around the map. Whenever one of them appeared headed toward the perimeter of his team's operational zone, a tech would issue orders through their hack into the PD computer system to reroute it. They'd been pushing the police away for fifteen minutes and probably had about that much time left before the chance of detection grew to unacceptable levels.

He said, "Getting close now."

His second-in-command, Natasha Kline, nodded. She'd wanted to be in the field for this one—*to be fair, she wants to be in the field for* every *mission*—but he'd instantly rejected that idea. It wasn't an appropriate adventure for her or the other magical on the team, Makka, to take part in.

Nonetheless, she wore her full combat gear in case she needed to portal to the location and get involved. *If that happens, things have seriously gone to hell, and we should retreat, anyway.*

One of the techs announced, "Squad A reports in position." Kevin returned his eyes to the monitors. The red tags that represented the four members of Squad A created a stationary cluster near the front of the house. Squads B and C were still in motion but had almost reached their designated destinations.

Each of his people was dressed in unidentifiable black fatigues for the operation, with body armor and backpacks for defense, and carried shotguns loaded with nonfatal ammunition. Each also bore some sort of Taser-inspired device, some of them modeled after pistols, others electrical nets that deployed from thrown canisters, and a bunch of simple shock grenades. The plan was to capture, rather than kill, their high-value target.

As he paced past her, he asked Tash, "Any last-minute concerns?"

He caught her scowl in his peripheral vision as she replied, "Yeah. I'm here rather than there. That's a mistake."

He huffed a small laugh, knowing she understood his

reasoning but still felt the need to grouse. "That particular question has been asked and answered to death. As the movie says, 'Let it go.'"

She sighed. "Whatever. Other than that incredibly poor choice on your part, it looks like our people will be in optimal strike points for the operation." She raised her voice. "Do we have the extra drones in position?"

Cassandra, their chief tech, replied, "Hovering nearby. If anyone attempts to move in on the target from any direction, we'll see them coming." She pointed at the highest row of monitors, positioned above the massive main displays. Each showed the feed from a drone, changing colors and images as the craft scanned through various detection modes.

One of the other techs announced, "Squad B in position."

Almost there. Kevin said, "I always knew having an oversight committee would be bad for business."

Tash's reply carried an extra dose of sarcasm. "Right. Or, maybe, you don't like the idea that someone's watching you. That you're accountable."

He rolled his eyes as he continued to pace. "Accountability is fine. Accountability to politicians, also mostly fine. Accountability to morons, that's an entirely different situation."

She laughed. "Well, you'll still have the morons after tonight."

He nodded. "If only our enemies had chosen one of them to visit, instead."

Left unmentioned was that a member of Sheen's team had almost certainly visited one of the morons, his private term for Senators Richardson and Borowski. That wasn't who they were interested in on this particular evening. While he'd love to see the two elected representatives from Nevada sent packing, their missteps hadn't yet ascended to the level of fraternizing with the enemy. *Unlike tonight's targets.*

His adrenaline spiked as the tech announced, "Squad C in position. Holding on your orders."

He activated his comm, which connected him to all his people. "All squads, clear to proceed. Stay safe. Do good." The last had become a frequent refrain for him, exhorting his team to perform well and reminding them that their mission served society. He and his team securely held the moral high ground. Although tonight's operation might be at the bottom edge of that lofty perch, it still wasn't climbing into the mud with the terrorists who were their ultimate targets.

Tash muttered, "I should be there."

He stopped his relentless movement and took a spot beside her, watching the screen. "No. I need you here. That's the burden of leadership, my friend."

"You suck."

The simple insult made him laugh despite the tension of the moment. "Not the first time someone's told me that. Doubtless won't be the last."

They both fell silent, eyes glued to the displays as tiny figures moved toward the front and back of the row house, ready to strike a blow against those who threatened their country.

Senator Aaron Finley laid down his cards with a grin. "Gin."

Bryant sighed and threw his cards down in disgust, having been only one turn away from making the same claim himself. He added up the values of the multiples and sequences on the table, since tonight they were playing to five hundred, and looked at his watch. *Maybe I can get out of here before he officially beats me. Call it a draw.*

"Is it time for another simulated failure?" They'd been playing cards to kill time between Finley's deactivation of the anti-magic emitter in the house. The senator had been feigning problems with the unit and said he'd even brought in some government techs to examine it to enhance the illusion. It meant that Bryant had to stay for several hours during each visit.

Not a particularly onerous task. Aaron's got good whiskey and is a fine conversationalist. All in all, I'd rather be back at the castle, though.

The conversion of the underground space on Pollepel Island had gone swiftly, taking less than a week to change from an empty shell to reasonable comfort. Ruby Achera's Mist Elf friends would continue improving the site, but it was already a functional base of operations. They'd chosen to call it "The Castle" in reference to Bannerman's Castle, the decrepit structure that was the island's most notable feature.

Bryant shuffled the cards, pulling the cuffs of his dress shirt back as he did. He'd worn a suit to visit his old friend, more for Finley's comfort than his since the senator would probably be a little nonplussed to see him in full combat gear again. Besides, this visit was one of the regularly scheduled meetings, not an emergency request, so he preferred to keep things casual.

Finley rose from his seat with a groan and nodded. "Yeah, I think we're good. Now, where the hell did I put that remote?" He wandered out of the dining room into the connected living room.

Bryant returned the cards to their wooden storage case, smiling a little at the fact that the back of each was personalized with the senator's initials, as was the box. *Probably a gift from a lobbyist.* Finley's voice came from the other room. "It's off."

Bryant stood and finished the ice melt in his whiskey. "All right. Thanks, my friend. I'll see you soon." He waved and muttered the appropriate incantation, reaching for his magic to open a portal back to the castle. When the magical throughway failed to materialize, he chuckled and called, "Aaron, did you hit the wrong button?"

Breaking glass and shouts, one of them a screech of alarm from his host, provided a most unexpected answer to his question.

CHAPTER TWO

As the noise of the home invasion sounded all around, Bryant ran to the living room to help his host. As soon as the chamber came into view, it was obvious he had no chance of success. Finley was already on the floor with a weapon trained on him and a figure kneeling on his back. Two more raised shotguns toward Bryant, and he took in the situation in an instant. Black uniforms for deniability. Black backpacks, familiar to him and his team, containing anti-magic emitters. *Which explains why I can't portal and severely limits my options.*

A gun hung suddenly heavy in his shoulder holster, loaded with anti-magic bullets, but shooting any of the invaders would risk crossing the line and killing them. In this chaos, he didn't trust he could shoot to wound. *Too much happening, too many people in motion.*

For a moment, he thought Finley, who he considered a friend, might've betrayed him. The horrified look the senator offered from his prone position reassured him that the other man was every bit as shocked as Bryant was.

His survival instincts finally kicked into gear. The sounds of breaking glass had all come from the first floor, so he dashed for the stairs. As he pounded up them, he cursed himself for not agreeing with Diana when she'd said he should always wear his full kit to visit Finley. *Here's where you pay the price for wanting some sense of normalcy in a world gone crazy, chucklehead.*

He rounded the corner and ran for the windows over-looking the house's tiny front yard. If he'd been planning the assault, he would've assumed anyone fleeing would choose the back and reinforced that area. *So, out the front it is.* The building's exterior was burned into his memory from countless hours of surveillance before he'd made initial contact after the attack on the vimana. So, when he crashed through the bedroom windows, he already knew his feet would land on the small roof that covered the doorway.

The leap from there to the yard was about twelve feet. Bryant hit hard, rolled, and came up running, quickly accelerating to top speed. *Maybe I can outrun the backpacks.* The streetlights were all extinguished, the neighborhood shrouded in darkness. Sounds of breaking glass from behind signaled pursuit by those who'd been inside the house. *Damn, damn, damn.*

He tested his magic continually, attempting to summon a small flame in his hand, but it resolutely failed to come. *They've gotten smart, have fast people on the chase to be sure the backpacks stay close. Need to remember to warn Diana about that.* Bryant came to a corner and turned right, trying to outguess his opponents by not moving directly away from their initial target. If he could get into the lane behind the houses, he'd sneak back toward the brownstone on the assumption it was the one place they wouldn't look for him.

Less than a minute later, that course of action was rendered impossible by a dark truck parked on the narrow road. He cursed and kept running past the alley. He was surprised at the unexpected lack of gunfire. It seemed like those pursuing him had as much interest in keeping their battle quiet as he did. *Or they've got something else in mind.*

The thought had barely completed before a drone whipped out of nowhere and ejected a series of canisters in his path. He accelerated reflexively, finding speed he didn't know he had and dove over them. They exploded right behind him, at least one sizzling with electricity that caught his lower leg and numbed it, sending a wave of pain up to his head. He stumbled, fell, and crawled away from the gas cloud created by another.

Bryant forced himself up and grabbed the back of his belt. Anyone noticing that part of his wardrobe would likely be surprised by the engraved discs that adorned it. It had been necessary to explain them away once or twice. He'd claimed he needed a bit of style in his government uniform, which had done the trick. However, the flattish circles were more than they appeared to be.

He grabbed one of the stun discs and palmed it, pressing on the appropriate spot to prime it. When the drone came in for a second pass, he hurled his projectile at it. The built-in accelerometer armed the disc as it flew, and the device activated when it reached an effective distance from the drone. It detonated in a wreath of technological lightning that encompassed his target. The craft angled into a deep dive and slammed into the ground a dozen feet away.

Bryant lurched back into motion, his leg now tingling painfully rather than completely numb, and grabbed another of the discs. He still limped, and his breath was coming harder than he'd like, but he doggedly kept moving. A commercial area lay only a couple of blocks ahead, and it would give him options if he could reach it. His comm continued to feed him static, the jamming that had activated when the invaders hit the house still active. *Resourceful bastards.*

He pulled out his phone on the run and hit the buttons to summon an autonomous car to one of those businesses. If he could make it there ahead of his pursuers, he should be able to use the vehicle to escape. As soon as he escaped the range of the backpacks, he'd portal to safety. Another drone swooped in suddenly, and he veered to the left to avoid it, cursing as it redirected him from his planned path with a familiar scattering of canisters.

You told them right where you were with the phone, dumb ass. He considered throwing it away but shoved it back in his pocket. Despite his initial self-accusation, he realized they'd almost certainly already known where he was since they likely had aerial surveillance on him. His use of the device probably wasn't what had allowed the drone to target him.

He reached an intersection, dropped the disc, and cut back toward the residential neighborhood, hoping to reach an alley and break into a house to hide. The munition exploded in a shower of glittering particles and smoke, hiding him momentarily from his pursuers' vision and sensors. *Hopefully.*

He cut into the alley, looking for a house with its trash barrel still out. Garbage collection had been days before so an empty container would signal a temporarily unoccupied home. He found one, dashed through the backyard, and pressed his phone against the electronic lock. The code-cracking software inside the device did its work, and the door popped open a moment later.

Bryant entered a kitchen, closed the door, and slumped to the floor in front of a cupboard. The room had two windows, one above and behind him and the other positioned symmetrically on the opposite side of the door. A pair of openings led from the room. One went to what looked like a hallway and the other to what was probably another room.

He controlled his breathing, continuing to test whether his magic had returned. Sustained failure suggested that his pursuers were still nearby, as did the static in his ear.

He pulled a small disc from the back of his watch, opened a cupboard, and pressed the clear magnetic object against a pan inside. The emergency beacon would begin sending a signal on a rarely used frequency to alert Diana to his predicament. He wouldn't use the cell for that. There was too much chance of them tracing the call. *Hell, the whole operation might've been an effort to get me to do that.*

When they breached the house, they did it perfectly. Breaking glass sounded from all over the first level. He saw the heat signatures in his glasses as people vaulted in and took up cover positions in other rooms, presumably aiming toward his location. The fact that they hadn't entered through the back once again suggested they were more interested in capturing him than killing him. *Which, right at the moment, at least gives me a chance.*

His phone rang, and he frowned at it. *Unknown number.* With a mental sigh and a physical shrug, he thumbed the accept button. A male voice came out of the speaker. "Bates. Kevin Serrano here. Time for you to give up."

"You're the scumbag in charge of this little militia."

The other man laughed. "I think they'd reject that classification. But yeah, I'm the decider, as they say. If you're wondering, we've had your digits for a while. Seems like the right occasion to use them."

Bryant asked, "Is Aaron okay?"

"Finley? Some bumps and bruises. Nothing more."

"I wouldn't have expected him to betray me." It was a blatant effort to get information, and the other man failed to oblige.

Serrano replied, "We face the unexpected here daily. So, like I said, it's time for you to come in. You'll be treated as a guest, within reason, of course."

Bryant asked, "No torture?"

The voice on the phone chuckled. "Maybe some light interrogation. Nothing that would violate the Geneva conventions. We're the good guys. We don't do that kind of garbage."

He snorted. "You're delusional."

The other man's voice hardened. "And you're either a terrorist yourself or at the very least shielding terrorists." He paused and continued with what seemed like more control, "Here's what's going to happen. You set down your weapons, including whatever gadgets you're carrying, and lie down on the floor with your hands on your head. We've got drones watching you, so we'll know if you do it or not. If you don't, we'll get you anyway, but it will probably hurt more. Rest assured, we brought along the right tools for the job."

Bryant shook his head. "If you think I have any choice here, you don't know my team or me very well." He killed the call and grabbed the other two discs on his belt. He threw them both through the room's exits, a flash-bang and the stun grenade, then climbed on the counter to dive out the back window and start running again.

The Taser net closed over him before he made it out. He fell badly into the backyard, his muscles refusing to obey his commands. The sick pain of a broken bone radiated up from his arm when he landed on it. Then, mercifully, the electricity overwhelmed his senses, and he lost consciousness.

CHAPTER THREE

The alert in her comm caused Diana to shoot out of bed, essentially transitioning from complete sleep to a full run in a matter of seconds. Rath and Max were a step behind her as she exited the small house that served as her quarters, located in one of the many tunnels attached to the main room of the cavern. She turned in the direction of the techs' working space, figuring that's where any useful information would be.

When she burst into the cabin to find both Kayleigh and Deacon in their chairs, typing furiously, she snapped, "Who, and where?" Her hands autonomously checked the pistols she'd grabbed automatically on the way out of her house, ensuring they were loaded and ready for action. She already knew *who*, as only two members of their team were absent from the base under Pollepel Island, and Sloan had signaled earlier that he was in for the night. Kayleigh confirmed her conclusion. "Bryant. D.C. Drones on the move."

Diana nodded, hot rage building inside her, tempered

with cold deliberation. To save her colleague, her boyfriend, she might have to cross the line and take someone out. For that, she'd do it if needed and to hell with the consequences. "Give me someplace specific so I can portal nearby."

Deacon replied quietly, "Your own rule, Boss. No one goes solo."

She countered, "I'm never alone with Rath around."

The troll said, "I'll get my gear," and ran off with the Borzoi at his side.

Kayleigh growled, "You can take it down a notch, Boss. According to the information that downloaded, the beacon's been going off for fifteen minutes. Whatever was happening when it turned on, it's almost certainly over."

Diana was fairly sure that the tech's anger wasn't directed at her, but it still made her fingers twitch with the desire to respond as if it was. She shoved the pistol she was holding into the waistband of her pants along her spine. "Why did we just hear it?"

"Jamming," Kayleigh snapped.

Diana had been so focused on other things that she hadn't noticed the arrival of her second-in-command at her back until the other woman spoke. Cara said, "So, best case, there's nothing to be seen there. Worst case, it's a trap."

The main screen in front of Kayleigh's workstation switched to show the feed from a drone flying over Georgetown. Sloan had arranged the rental of several spaces in Washington, and Deacon and Kayleigh had positioned drones in them on the assumption they'd eventually need resources to deal with Serrano and his team. The craft were consumer models with some additional tech added, which gave them a bit of anonymity in the comings and goings of uncrewed vehicles in Washington's airspace.

The drone approached a brownstone with D.C. Police Department vehicles arrayed on the street in front of it, and officers spread out in the front and back. Diana asked, "Finley's house? Is he okay?"

Kayleigh answered, "Not his. Another one, several blocks away. No information on Finley."

Cara suggested, "Call in a tip. Have them check out his place too."

Deacon replied, "On it."

The drone had to stay high above the vehicles the police were using for their aerial views of the space. Kayleigh asked, "Deke, do those cops look like they're wearing body cameras to you?"

"Yeah, good idea. Stand by." A dozen seconds later, the infomancer continued, "Okay. I'm in."

The monitor in front of his workstation split into a grid of cameras, presumably worn by the police at the scene. Most were in motion, not showing anything particularly useful. The audio chatter that came with them, on the other hand, provided some new information. It sounded like one of the officers must've been near the investigating detectives to judge by the content it was sharing.

A voice said, "Looks like a fight happened here. Someone was in this room, came in through the back door. Then went out the window when people broke in the front."

Another responded, "That's consistent with what the outside shows. Found some blood there, too."

"Enough for a bleed out?"

"Nah. Minor stuff."

The sudden twist that had taken over Diana's stomach relaxed. She said, "Okay. Everyone into main, right now. Bring Sloan in, too." She turned and strode out of the small cabin toward the large Quonset hut that served as their operations center. Rath and Max rejoined her on the way, the troll wearing his throwing knives, batons, protective vest, and flight gear.

Cara, walking at her side, said softly, "Keep it calm, Boss. Can't just react. That's what they want. Think it through."

Her second was frightfully good at reading her emotional state, and Diana forced herself to blow out a long breath. "Don't worry. I'm not going to run in without a plan. But I'm definitely thinking. Believe me, I'm thinking hard."

Her team had all heard the alert, so she didn't have to wait long for them to arrive. The normal mirth and positivity they shared were absent. She sat on the edge of a table to keep herself from pacing and said, "So. It's bad. Bryant has presumably fallen into enemy hands. We're not sure if Finley betrayed him, if they took him too, or what.

"The police found blood at the scene of what we presume was Bryant's capture, based on where he left his emergency beacon, but not enough to be fatal. So, we'll proceed on the assumption that he's alive and Serrano has captured him."

Hank asked, "Should we pack up to abandon the base?" He scowled. "It's almost livable, finally." The dark joke fell flat.

Diana replied, "Being underground has its advantages. No reason to leave yet. As far as I know, even if Serrano does find out where we are, he doesn't have any heavy weapons to bring to bear. He's not the Army. We can handle whatever punishment a drone can deliver as long as we have people here to throw up shields.

"I want full coverage at all times. Drones up on every vector at distance intervals to ensure we have as much alert as possible. Buy every drone you need to make it happen."

Kayleigh and Deacon nodded. Diana continued, "That's surveillance. For defense, find the best spots on the surface to take out any incoming drones with magic or weapons."

Tony observed, "So we're turning our castle into one in truth."

Diana confirmed, "As surreptitiously as possible. At any sign of real trouble, we portal out before they can get their damn anti-magic emitters running. I mean that seriously. If anyone who's not us makes it to the island's surface, the defenders on top bug out, and people down below portal away.

"Khan, wire up anything we wouldn't want our enemies to have. Small scale, limited effect, only the amount needed to do the job. Last one out can blow it. Cara, oversee shielding a building, the one farthest from the surface. We want to block the anti-magic emitters' signals if we can. Cost is no object. Put it on one of the government credit cards we've cracked."

The two she'd just given orders looked at each other, then nodded their understanding.

Diana made sure to meet the eyes of each team member as she continued talking. "On top of all that, we need supplies, and we need intel. Sloan, Kayleigh, Deacon, and I will work on gathering information. Hank, Tony, and Rath, figure out where we can get some serious gear fast for taking these bastards on toe-to-toe and for defending ourselves here."

She clapped once, appreciating the focused looks on every face in the room. "Okay. We're on the clock to rescue Bryant before they can break him. Move."

CHAPTER FOUR

W hen her people had departed to their tasks, Diana paused long enough to fill a large travel mug with coffee before heading back to the techs' cabin. Deacon had only arrived the day before after Hank and Kayleigh had secured Internet access that would be mostly adequate to his needs.

They'd gotten the satellite connection running several days before. He hadn't been willing to relocate until they'd also arranged a wireless hack into an optical fiber line a couple of miles away. That task had required some specialized equipment and taken some extra time.

Now they were all together. *Except Bryant. We're going to fix that.* Diana surveyed the setup as she walked into the center of the room. She hadn't seen it since Deacon's arrival aside from her hasty earlier visit when she'd been rather focused on other things.

Each tech had low monitors on the desk in front of them in a standard computer setup. Each also had several monitors of various sizes mounted on the walls above them. Diana stood in the middle and looked around, then chuckled. "Not quite the Pit, is it?"

Kayleigh laughed at the reference to their old base in Pittsburgh. "Hardly. But we have Deacon now, so I guess that makes up for the loss of fancy tech."

He snorted. "I've never worked with such an iffy connection. Satellite? Wireless to fiber?" He shook his head. "It's enough to give me nightmares."

Diana shrugged. "Come up with a better idea, and I'll be happy to make it happen."

Kayleigh said, "He's whining. He enjoys it. Gives his life purpose."

She replied, "Here's a purpose. Let's see what the D.C. traffic cameras had on Finley's house leading up to the attack." She barely made out Deacon's muttered, "Stupid monkey," as he hit the buttons to call up the traffic cameras. "What?"

He sighed. "Never mind." A few more keystrokes and the monitors above him filled with images of cars and stoplights. A map highlighting the cameras they were looking at with Finley's house in the center showed in one of them. As he rewound the feeds, he said, "We'll go back an hour before the beacon went off." The cameras nearest the senator's residence were on the big monitor, and he fast-forwarded through their recordings.

Kayleigh had spun her chair around to watch, and Diana sipped her coffee as the images whipped by. Max pushed into the room and sat beside her, leaning his weight against her leg. She'd been the dog's friend first, but once Rath appeared, he'd become the canine's favorite person. Clearly, the Borzoi knew a little emotional support would be welcome at the moment. She reached down, scratched his head, and whispered, "We'll get him back, Maxie. Don't you worry."

Finally, they arrived at the timestamp when the beacon began transmitting, with no evidence of cars at Finley's place. Deacon asked, "Do you want to go through again?"

Diana shook her head. "It makes sense they would portal in. It's safer, doesn't risk discovery until the last minute, and we know Serrano's got magicals on his team. Let's do the same thing at the location where the beacon was."

The infomancer made it happen, and they repeated the process of scanning through the recording. This time, a large van appeared on the cameras, seemingly headed toward the house. Diana said, "Too bad we don't have any feeds that point at the house, the street in front of it, or the alley behind it. Any other resources we can tap for that?"

Kayleigh offered, "Security cameras in the houses, maybe?"

"I already have backdoors into all the security companies. They were way easier than the stupid traffic cameras." Deacon muttered again, this time too low to hear, then said, "Okay. Looks like we've got a hit."

Cameras from across the street showed a large black van pulling up outside the house in question around when the beacon would've started signaling, unaware jamming prohibited it from reaching anyone useful. They saw a hooded figure dragged across the lawn in handcuffs, staggering a bit and favoring one arm. People in black fatigues threw Bryant roughly into the back of the vehicle. Diana recognized him from his outfit, build, and the way he moved. The van immediately pulled away.

Kayleigh said, "I wonder why they didn't portal him out of there?"

Diana had counted on them making that decision since a portal would've left them no clues to follow. "It wouldn't have been smart to risk having Bryant able to use his magic when they dropped the blockers to create their portal. That's why they could use magic to deploy around Finley's house but needed a ride to take Bryant away. Sure, they could have knocked him out, but that carries risks. This was simpler, and they would've had no idea we had camera access."

She took another sip of coffee. "Okay. Kayleigh, you run the cameras forward and find out where that van went. Deke, let's go back to Finley's cameras and see if we can find a similar van anywhere nearby."

Several minutes later, they'd discovered that indeed a second van of a similar model had been driving around Finley's house. Grabbing the feeds from the nearby security cameras from his neighbors' houses showed that he, too, had been bundled into it. They traced both vehicles back to a nondescript garage in an industrial area of town.

For the first time since the alarm went off, hope grew in Diana. "Okay. Watch that spot for the next two hours. If they go on the move, a drone goes with them. If we don't see any activity to convince us otherwise, we'll hit it.

"I doubt it's their main base unless fate is *way* more on our side than usual. If it were me, I'd probably have planned to drug Bryant and Finley, then portal them someplace useful. Who knows, we might get lucky."

Kayleigh snorted. "Yeah, we're overflowing with luck lately."

Deacon countered, "Now who's the whiner?"

Max barked at them, and Diana managed a chuckle. "That's right, Maxie, they should both shut up and get to work. Deacon, I'd like you to check the network enhancers, make sure they're good to go. If we find a connection at the garage to Serrano's systems, that would be the next best thing to finding Bryant there."

She sighed and looked down at Max. "All righty. Let's leave these folks to their work and go chat with Sloan about backup plans in case we don't find anything."

When Diana and Max had departed, Deacon sighed. "Those enhancers are fine. We've checked them a zillion times."

Kayleigh stood and stepped behind him, her surprisingly strong hands kneading his shoulders. "Check anyway. If the boss wants it done, there's a reason."

He closed his eyes and leaned back, relaxing. "Yeah, to keep me busy with useless things."

"Maybe she's tired of your complaining. What exactly do you have against primates?"

Deacon scowled, thinking back to his hack into the D.C. traffic camera network, which had involved playing a virtual version of Donkey Kong where he was Mario. "It's not worth discussing. I'll check the emitters. You keep an eye around the garage."

Kayleigh laughed and returned to her chair. "Might

need you to portal in and drop off some extra drones once you finish."

"Fine." He left the cabin, headed for the main building where the arming room and equipment stockpiles were. *Stupid monkey. Stupid barrels. Stupid overalls. When this is over, I'm gonna reprogram their damn system, so anytime they want to log in they have to play Donkey Kong.*

CHAPTER FIVE

Bryant remembered falling out the window and hitting the ground with a recollection so fresh it almost hurt. Fuzzier was his memory of being taken, the hood going over his head, the walk to the van. He figured they'd hit him with some sort of light sedative right away. The way they'd thrown him into the vehicle was still entirely fresh due to the incredible pain he'd felt when he landed on his broken arm.

Then, for a time, his mental file was completely blank, as if the movie of his life had faded to black and only faded up at this precise moment. He was sitting upright, his head hanging down on his chest. An attempt to summon his magic failed, as he'd expected it would. He focused on listening but heard nothing more than ordinary HVAC noises and maybe the edge of some muffled conversation.

Forcing open sticky eyes, he confirmed what his ears told him. The surrounding area was a smallish room, the size of a standard office. Sweatpants and a sweatshirt had replaced his suit, and cold shackles at his ankles bound his legs to the metal chair under him.

Bryant peered down and saw that the seat was bolted to the floor, as was the metal table in front of him. His arms rested on its surface. Handcuffs threaded through a large bolt welded onto the table kept them there. He flexed his muscles, discovering that they'd healed his arm while he was unconscious. *That's something, anyway.*

The rest of the room was sterile and boring. White painted walls, a wooden door, and another metal chair across the table from him. He and Diana had assumed Serrano was probably working out of a generic office building somewhere since their search of government records hadn't shown his presence in any of their facilities, and this space reinforced that conclusion.

Could it be someone other than Serrano? He considered the question and judged that no one else would've had the knowledge and logistical support to undertake the operation that had captured him. *I hope Aaron's okay.*

His mind held no suspicion of his friend, not given the way the invaders had treated him and the shocked look that had appeared on his face. Of course, a good actor could pull all that off, so he wouldn't *act* upon that trust without verifying it first. Still, inside his head, he was confident the senator hadn't betrayed him.

The door handle turned with a *click*, and a woman walked in and introduced herself. "I'm Tash. You're going to answer some questions for me."

He managed a grin, more at the absurdity of the situation than in any real amusement. "Natasha Kline. Been with Serrano for a while. Nice to see you in person, rather than as a photo on a page. Might've hoped for better circumstances, though."

"Don't try to flirt. You're not good at it. Plus, you're a scumbag." She sat across from him, opened the file folder she'd brought, and spread his records out on the table. "It's always sad when someone with so much positive contribution to his government, someone who could almost be called a hero, turns traitor."

Bryant shook his head. "You can't possibly be that stupid. You know we're not traitors."

She shrugged. "Your actions were not to the benefit of your government, and it's an easy jump from there to say they were harmful to it. How else would you define being a traitor?"

"If those things were true, I'd agree with you. They're not."

She leaned back and crossed her arms. "So, you deny that your team failed to turn over all the artifacts you found following established procedures?"

He shrugged with the limited motion the cuffs allowed. "Established procedures don't really apply when you're in as variable and dire a situation as we are with the artifacts." He lifted an eyebrow. "Seems as if you all are taking a page from that same book, as well."

Kline offered him a thin smile. "*We* do what our government tells us to do. We're not doing anything more than exactly what they've given us authority to do. Unlike you."

"Potayto, potahto."

She sighed. "The whole delaying thing you're doing? It won't work. We found your embedded locator with an xray and cut it out. Not that it would've worked here, anyway. If your friends are stupid enough to follow it, they'll walk right into a trap."

He locked his face down so it wouldn't react. In truth, he'd figured that they'd jam the device implanted in his calf, but using it as bait was an annoyingly competent move on their part. Hopefully, they hadn't realized it needed to be activated by a specific sequence of signals from his watch. "Well, I'm not going to answer any of your questions, so I guess you can toddle along and tell your boss that you failed."

Kline leaned forward. "Luckily for you, he was unwilling to let our magic people go one-on-one with you. We would've cleaned your clock."

"I suppose if your boss had any real faith in you, you would've had the chance. What do you think that says about your relationship?"

The door opened again, and a laughing man came walking in. "Okay, Tash, enough. Now he's being a jerk."

She rose from the seat. "I know. Thanks for letting me have a conversation with him beforehand."

Serrano, who he recognized from his file picture, nodded as the woman left the room. He took her place in the chair across the table, swinging his leg over the back to sit down rather than pulling it out. His smile was annoyingly arrogant. "So, here we are. Number one guy of the good guys, number one guy of the bad guys."

Bryant rolled his eyes. "Do you hear your own theme music in your head, too, hero?"

The other man laughed, seeming honestly amused. "You know, sometimes I do. I think we *all* do. Let's get to business. What was your girlfriend planning to do with the artifacts she was keeping behind?"

Bryant shrugged. "Pretty sure her only goal was to keep them out of the hands of people who would misuse them."

"Seems like that's not her call to make. What's she going to do with the ones she has now? Use them to power up your team?"

He scowled. "If you think those things are 'power-ups,' you're both paranoid and stupid. Rhazdon artifacts are a menace. No one who wants one should be allowed to have one."

Serrano gave a sharp nod. "We agree on that. Which is why someone trustworthy should lock them away, not have them held by some renegade bureau leader."

"Are you talking about Diana or yourself?"

The other man chuckled. "Touché. Don't deflect. *You* think Sheen should've turned them over, too."

Bryant shook his head. "I support her decisions, one hundred percent. Your little bunch of foot soldiers here is enough evidence of the need to be *very* careful about where those things go."

Serrano changed tactics suddenly. "Where's the team hiding out? Now that you don't have the vimana, are you being forced to rely on old friends? Ruby Achera, maybe?"

"Please. There's no way in hell I'll give you any information that will lead you to my team."

The other man shrugged. "Okay, how about this? What's the deal with the cult? Is Sheen looking to take over as the leader? Trying to steal the artifacts? That one came out of the blue; I've gotta tell you. If I were leading your team, I'd hunker down out of sight."

Bryant nodded, wishing he could properly cross his arms and look down his nose at his captor. "I imagine you would. Fortunately, some of us believe in contributing to the greater good rather than hampering those trying to do so."

"As you see it."

"Everything's subjective. That's why the bad guy in the movie always believes they're the good guy. In case that was too subtle, I'm talking about you."

He thought that insult might've landed, but Serrano simply shifted to a new topic. "What other members of the government have you compromised in addition to Finley? We know about your team's move on Richardson, for example."

Bryant couldn't stop himself from flinching at the mention of the senators' names and knew he'd given away something he would've rather kept secret. He replied, "I think I've finished chatting with you, Kev. It was lovely to meet you. You'd better toddle off. I'm sure your henchmen are looking for orders."

Serrano shook his head. "I'm afraid you don't get to decide when the interview is over." He opened the case and turned it so Bryant could see what was inside, then removed the automatic injector. He stood, came around to Bryant's formerly broken arm, and gripped it with one hand. When the other depressed the plunger, the needle stabbed into his arm hard enough to hurt.

"The drug won't take too long to do its work. Then you'll tell me everything I want to know. There shouldn't be any lasting damage, but no way to be positive, I'm afraid." He returned the device to the case, closed it, and picked it up. "I'm going to go grab a coffee. You want anything?" Bryant didn't reply, and Serrano shrugged. "Suit yourself."

After he'd left, Bryant drew a deep breath and hoped that they'd only x-rayed him, not subjected him to an MRI. Each of his agents had a capsule embedded above their collarbone that would render them unconscious for a time. It wasn't a particularly well-known drug and thus shouldn't be easily countered by whatever Serrano and his people had on hand. *Of course, depending on what he shot into me, the interactions could be less than wonderful.*

He swallowed his concern, knowing that if something *did* happen to him, but his action protected the rest of his team, that was a trade he'd make every single time. He pulled against the cuffs and leaned forward, then dug his fingers into the appropriate spot. He ground them into the muscle and surrounding area to be sure he broke the capsule open until he felt the hazy flood of one or both of the drugs at work.

The only thought in his mind as his consciousness started to fade was of Diana and how ticked off she'd be that he'd gotten himself captured. *I'm never going to hear the end of it.*

CHAPTER SIX

Diana strode through the operations area of the main building, passed through the training space that occupied most of the back half, and finally arrived in the section that held their equipment storage and lockers. It was clean and brightly lit, and its purity always helped her focus her mind on impending action. It was the one place in the underground complex she'd insisted be replicated from their previous bases, imagining that her team would find the familiarity as soothing as she did.

Most of her people had arrived before her, including Rath and Max. She shook her head at the troll but couldn't hold back the smile that accompanied it. "Do you really think we should bring Maxie along on this one, buddy?"

He nodded. "Definitely. Max is one of us." He said the last trio of words like the characters in *Freaks*, a movie that Kayleigh had shown him despite Diana's refusal to do so.

Diana shrugged. His insistence on the Borzoi being a more active part of their team didn't seem to bother the dog, and she'd learned to trust his instincts in most cases. *Other than movie selections.* "Okay. You're in charge of keeping him safe. Be sure he wears his vest and put Tasers in the holsters."

Rath grinned. "Roger Roger."

Her reflexive response was somewhere between a laugh and a groan. "Your battle droid impression is sharp, buddy. Maybe find something new to add to the repertoire, huh? That one is a little worn."

He stuck his tongue out at her, drawing laughs from several of the other agents. Diana opened her locker and paused to collect herself, closing her eyes and focusing inward. In her mind, she took the concerns of the moment, things not directly pertinent to the battle to come, and shoved them into mental lockers. She imagined the locks *clicking* shut, trapping them securely inside where they wouldn't distract her.

It required a lot of shoving to get her concern for Bryant stowed away, but she managed it. *Doesn't help him or me to worry about that right now.* When it was all locked down, she drew a deep breath in through her nose and let it out through her mouth, consciously shifting into combat mode. When her eyes opened again, she was focused and ready.

She'd already donned her tactical pants and uniform shirt over the base layer of her outfit. The equipment belt went next, and she secured its tie-down holster around her right thigh. Diana ran her hands along the wide belt, mentally cataloging each piece of gear on it by size, shape, and grooves carved into it. Those notches allowed the team to differentiate between one kind of grenade disc and another.

Next, she traded her everyday boots, the ones with throwing knives and a stiletto, for the version with a heftier dagger in the left boot and her backup pistol holster in the right. A Sig Sauer P238 went into it, loaded with seven anti-magic rounds. She hoped not to have to use it, but circumstances were pushing her toward the line where doing fatal damage might become necessary for her or her team's survival. In that circumstance, she'd do what she had to do.

Diana yanked the laces tight, stood from the stool she'd sat on, and pulled her vest from the locker. She slipped it on, securing the Velcro straps on the sides tightly, then slid her shock gloves over her hands, flexing her fists to make sure everything felt right. She crossed to the charging station and picked up the power cell that fed the gloves, stashing it in its empty slot on her equipment belt. It was a moment's work to attach the line that ran through the base layer to it and to secure the small connectors that hung out of the suit's wrists to the gloves.

Miniature LEDs at the base of each glove winked for a second to confirm an active connection to the power supply. She'd talked with Kayleigh about reworking the system to allow for two batteries and thus more shock charges, but in the chaos of the move, they hadn't had time to test out the change. *Eventually, I guess. Until then, we'll make do.*

Next, she strapped on armor pads at shins and fore-arms, upper arms and thighs, elbows and knees. Her main pistol went into its holster, and she slid extra mags for the Glock into slots on her vest. Concern over their dwindling inventory of anti-magic bullets and magic deflector crystals pushed at the edges of her mind, and she shoved them into a mental locker with an inward snarl. *We have enough for tonight. Worry about that tomorrow.*

Finally, Diana pulled out Fury's harness and slipped it on. The sword itself generally stayed in her quarters or with her and currently rested against her locker's open door. She pulled it from its sheath, slid it into the one attached to the harness on her back, and stored the other in her locker. Now fully armed and ready to go, she closed the door and put on her best southern twang. "All right, all right, all right."

Cara, gearing up next to her, laughed. "Rath's not the only one who needs a new line, Boss. Everyone in the room knew we wouldn't get out of here without hearing your terrible Matthew McConaughey impression."

Diana frowned. "It's not bad." A chorus of voices assured her that indeed it was, and more that she should never do it again. She huffed in feigned annoyance. "Fine. Be that way."

She crossed to what she thought of as the weapons wall, where the team's heavier armaments resided. She pulled down one of the grenade launchers and checked the order of the canisters in the drum, advancing it until the lead munition was a flash-bang.

At first, she hadn't been a fan of the weapon. After using them on several occasions, she was now of the opinion that they did a solid job of thinning out the enemy with minimal potential loss of life. That was a good thing in most situations.

When they got out of their current predicament, she'd look into getting the team a new primary rifle, something with an underslung grenade launcher, preferably magazine fed. It would be comparatively cumbersome, and they'd have to spend some time training to grow accustomed to the difference in weight and size, but she thought that having the option to be nonlethal would be a positive overall.

She attached it to the strap on her vest and let it hang, then paced the room one slow step after the next as her team finished gearing up. She inspected each person's deflector crystal, ensuring it was completely clear and showed no sign of cracks. What awaited them in the garage was a mystery, and the knowledge that any surprise magical attacks would get sucked away safely by the gemstones offered deep reassurance.

She raised her voice so it would carry and announced, "We have three priorities for this mission. Number one, don't get killed." They laughed, and Hank quipped some-thing about her ridiculous expectations.

"Two, rescue Bryant and Finley. If they aren't on-site, our focus becomes gathering intel. Only fight when you have to and keep it nonlethal. Better that we retreat rather than kill someone, again, unless our people are there."

Cara asked, reluctance in her tone, "What if only the senator is present?"

"We don't cross the line for Finley. If we spot him and need to bail, we'll call the police and the Secret Service. Kayleigh, set that up."

Over the comm, the tech replied, "Will do, boss."

Diana finished, "Three, keep your eyes on the prize. Our people or intel to take us the next step of the way. We're all emotional on this one, but we can't let it distract us. Any questions?" None were forthcoming, and she nodded in satisfaction. "Okay. Let's do it."

CHAPTER SEVEN

Sloan had secured an insertion site a couple of blocks away from the garage during the two hours they'd waited and watched. Now he called up a portal, and the team passed through it. The industrial neighborhood contained a strange mix of high buildings next to squat ones, with streets that seemed wider than they needed to be and a sort of orange tint thrown by the streetlights coloring everything. It was decidedly odd, or in Rath's opinion, "Spooky."

Diana nodded. "I'm with you on that one, Rambo. It's like stepping onto an alien planet or something."

They moved as individual units with Diana, Rath, and Max leading the way. Hank, Anik, and Sloan were in the middle, and Cara and Tony brought up the rear.

As they advanced, the feed from a new drone appeared in her glasses to complement the overhead view they already had. This one flew at a much lower height and showed a structure that looked like an auto repair shop, with six closed garage doors on one long side. The building itself was only about two stories high, and she imagined the inside would have no second level, or maybe only a partial one. She asked, "We have any blueprints for this?"

Deacon replied, "Negative. The only records are for the empty shell of the construction, nothing useful on the interior."

The drone skimmed over the roof, revealing only HVAC equipment and no easy access. Diana said, "Not getting in that way. Highlight defenses." Their recon craft swung around for another pass, and cameras at the corners of the building took on a red overlay, as did a line of electrical signals that was probably an alarm system.

"Croft, when we get close, you take the far camera, and I'll deal with the near one. We'll use Barb's trick." Ruby Achera's sister, Morrigan, shared how she used illusion to create a kind of invisibility specifically to defeat cameras. They would make their approach under a veil, of course, but it never hurt to improve the odds of remaining undetected.

Cara replied, "Righto."

Diana pinched the bridge of her nose with her eyes closed. "Deke, you have the alarms under control?"

The infomancer responded, "Affirmative. I have the net connection isolated, and the jamming will take care of wireless. Fortunately, the phone is a VoIP, so even if they're using a hard line, my hack will block it."

"Activate jamming." The stationary drone above the building would put out a heavy signal blocker across a wide band. In addition, smaller modules on each of their belts would do the same. The techs had carefully programmed the devices to avoid blocking the primary or backup frequencies their comms used.

Diana said, "We'll do three doors. I have the nearest. Croft, the one beside mine. Hercules and Face, the next in line. Remember, stay nonfatal if we can." The repeated reminder annoyed even her, but it had to be said.

Confirmations came, then she gave the order. "Moving." She trotted out in front of the rest, headed for the door.

Maintaining the illusion for the camera and the veil concealing her, Rath, and Max required some concentration but wasn't otherwise taxing. She had enough brainpower and plenty of magic power remaining to reach out with her telekinesis and hurl the garage door upward, shattering whatever lock or block might've been in place to render it immobile.

Cara did the same for her assigned barrier. Hank's and Sloan's magics primarily specialized in a single area and thus were less powerful in others. They made their door creak and shudder, but it failed to rise. Diana dashed into the opening in front of her. "Forget the third door. Get inside. Same areas of responsibility."

Their sensors had already revealed heat signatures within the building, some seemingly milling around while others clustered. The people they represented lurched into motion at the sound of the garage doors crashing upward, and she grinned at the knowledge that they'd taken their enemies by surprise. Her zone of control was the left third of the space. That included a trio of figures rising from a small table they'd been sitting around and knocking the plates of food covering it to the floor.

Their instinctive move was to go for their weapons, and each had a rifle leaning against the wall nearby. Diana extended her telekinesis, grabbed the rifles, and hurled them as a bundle to land with a clatter behind her. The enemy troops reached for their pistols, and she pulled the trigger on her grenade launcher, dispatching a flash-bang followed immediately by stun and web grenades. They detonated one after the next, incapacitating two of the three.

Rath and his sidekick dashed forward, the dog a few steps faster than his partner. Max leapt up, closed his teeth around the arm that was trying to bring a pistol to bear, and dragged the weapon down so the man's shots went into the floor. With his foe's defense compromised, Rath darted in and stabbed him with his stun batons, the dual *snaps* dropping their enemy to the floor, semi-conscious and moaning. The troll silenced him with another jab.

Diana snapped, "Any alarm?"

Deacon replied, "Yeah, but it didn't get anywhere."

"Good. Now find me some damn intel, stat." She turned and dashed toward her teammates to help with their battles.

Cara and Tony entered their area and immediately came under fire from two directions, thanks to the third door's reluctance to rise. She reached out with her telekinesis and grabbed a pair of heavy rolling toolboxes, rusty enough that they were probably leftovers from whatever the garage had been in its prime, and positioned them in front of her and her partner to absorb the incoming rounds. In a normal fight, she'd throw them at the people with the rifles, but that could too easily be fatal. She said, "Gonna need you to step up, Stark."

He laughed. "My pleasure." He lifted his grenade launcher so the barrel was pointing over the toolboxes and pulled the trigger three times, sending grenades toward the enemies in front of them. The incoming fire from that direction slackened as they detonated, and he twisted and launched three more at the ones to the right.

Cara dropped the toolboxes as the incoming barrage stopped and ran at the foes ahead of them, leaping over the obstruction she'd created and rushing at one of the pair still standing. She snapped a front kick into the nearest one's stomach, then spun and landed a back fist on his partner's cheekbone. Her stun glove discharged, and the man collapsed with the *snap* of a broken bone. *Oops. So sorry.*

She continued her spin and charged at the one she'd kicked, who was still stumbling backward and trying to regain his balance. Cara thrust both hands forward in a double punch at his chest. Again, the gloves delivered a bolt of electricity, and he fell to the floor. The blow was too far from his brain to put him all the way out, so she gave him a gentle tap on the temple to finish the job.

Meanwhile, Tony had chosen a different plan that emphasized his strengths. His extra-large Desert Eagle pistol was in his hand, and he pulled the trigger calmly. His aim was perfect, as it always was. The enemy nearest him went down howling as the bullet smashed into their shin, likely breaking it despite the protective plate wrapped around it.

Tony switched his sights to the next and repeated the process to a similar effect. Luckily for the third, he'd fallen to the web grenade and was no longer a threat. Cara observed, "Hercules, you're late for the party. Stark took care of yours for you."

Hank complained, "Not fair. You owe me."

Tony laughed. "I'd say that's the other way around, buddy."

Diana ordered, "Spread out and look for anything that will give us a direction to go. Clearly, they didn't keep their captives here, so we need to find a clue." When Cara reached the back wall, her sensor pack revealed another area behind it.

She mentioned it, and Deacon replied, "Get an enhancer down for me, please." Cara complied, setting the small equipment brick on a nearby shelf. A moment later, he said, "Okay, I'm into the building's systems. Looks like there's something in the wall that blocks signals until you're close." Then, in a voice suddenly charged with alarm, he barked, "It's an ambush."

CHAPTER EIGHT

Diana brought her hands up with palms facing the facility's back wall, which had appeared to be the building's outer perimeter but wasn't, and blasted it with a double burst of force magic. The drywall and the studs underneath shattered, opening a hole for her to race through. She drew Fury with her right hand as she ran and hacked away the sharp-edged wood jutting into the hole as she crossed through.

The space was unexpectedly large, about half as big as the main garage section. Three portals were in the process of closing, and in front of each was a squad of five people in matching military-style armor. Four of them carried rifles, the nearest of which was already shifting in her direction. The last member of each group was unarmed but had a hand or wand raised to maintain a bubble of magical protection around their unit.

Her brain put the pieces together in an instant, and she shouted, "Physical shields." She reached out with her telekinesis and grabbed a toolbox from nearby, dragged it over, and crouched behind it. The soldiers fired from inside the bubble, their anti-magic rounds passing through it unhindered to slam into her protective metal cover.

She angled her launcher upward and sent a flash-bang grenade in a shallow arc. When it detonated, she launched shock and web, hoping the first would've taken out the magical. The lack of a decrease in incoming fire signaled the failure of that hope. She swore, then called, "Target the magicals. It's our only option. With their shields, only one choice exists. Stark, keep it to wounds, please."

Tony relaxed into his firing stance. Normally, this would be when he would make a joke, but instead, his focus had shifted entirely to the enemies in front of him. Cara spun metal objects of various sizes in a sphere around them, protecting them from incoming bullets. He activated the thermal display in his glasses and aimed at the leg of the nearest magical. It was easy to identify the ones not shooting a weapon by their posture.

He said, "Give me a hole," and an opening appeared a moment later in the defensive screen. He squeezed the trigger the instant the hole was large enough, burying a round in the nearest enemy magical's leg. The heavy caliber bullet entered beside the body armor that protected the limb. The person fell, as did the defensive shield.

Cara hurled several heavy objects from their protective screen at the men with the rifles, forcing them to scatter. Their dispersal opened Tony's firing lanes to the other two magicals, and he smoothly shot each of them in the leg as well. The one nearest Hank, Anik, and Sloan managed to keep his shield up, but the other flickered and vanished. Tony bolted to the side and dove into cover as rifle bullets zipped through the air near him. Finally, he had a free moment for a quip. "I don't think they like me very much."

Hank growled, "No one likes you, Stark." He'd found a car hood and held it up in front of him like a battering ram as he ran at the nearest enemies. Bullets slammed into it, pounding dents into the hunk of metal. He hoped it was thick enough to last for as long as he needed.

Fortunately, that wasn't long, and it did. Three shooters dove out of the way before he reached them, but he rammed the fourth and sent him flying. He dropped the slab and shuffle-stepped to the left, where one of the men was lifting his rifle. Hank punched him in the stomach with his left fist, slammed the man's ribs with his right, and smashed another left into the side of his foe's face, twisting his hips and putting momentum into the blow.

The first pair of blows struck body armor but hurt, judging by his enemy's looks of pain. The third sent him to the floor from the force of the impact and a shock glove detonating on an unprotected area. Magic built inside Hank with each punch, and he hoarded it carefully, not yet finding a threat that required spending it.

Anik and Sloan had engaged the other two and were wrestling with them, focused on keeping their guns out of play. *Just like we agreed, good work guys.*

In this arrangement, their only role was to stay safe

and do their best to control the enemy while Hank delivered the destruction. He strode in and brought down the closer one before he had a chance to realize a new threat had joined the fight. The other kicked Sloan in the stomach and backpedaled, turning and raising his fists at Hank.

He laughed. "Really?"

The other man, who was well-built but not nearly as muscular as Hank, nodded. "Let's go. One-on-one, you and me."

"Not here to play games with you, friend. Khan?" His partner pulled the trigger, and a stun grenade went off at the man's feet. He stuttered and jerked, then collapsed. Hank shook his head at the fallen figure. "Tie him up while I see if there's anyone else worth taking on."

When Tony shot the magical in their group, Rath dashed in with his batons. He leaped and landed in the center of the four men with rifles. The troll swung his weapons with reckless abandon, not aiming, sacrificing technique for pure speed and power. They slammed into flesh on all sides, eliciting shouts, moans of pain, and a lot of cursing as the men tried to figure out what was going on. He laughed as he continued to hack and slash.

His acrobatic entry had surprised them enough to knock them off balance, and the fact that their opponent was only three feet tall contributed to their continuing confusion. The first one to gain perspective and try to bring his rifle down got the point of Rath's baton in the groin. A scream of pain followed the loud *snap*, and Rath laughed harder.

One of them falling away gave the rest a little more space to react, though, and the second shifted out of Rath's melee range as a prelude to shooting. Max took care of him with a flying leap to slam into the man. His teeth latched onto the rifle strap that secured it to his foe's armor and yanked it hard. The bullets went into the air as the canine wrestled the human down to the floor.

Diana arrived in time to deal with the third, slamming him in the back of his shoulders with the flat of her sword and propelling him forward. Rath, who'd seen her coming, swiped his batons in and up at the man's shins, upending him. He hit the floor with a crash that made the troll wince.

The fourth paused, unsure which threat to face first. Rath threw his baton like a spear. Its stun tip caught the man in the neck and dropped him. The troll shook his head at the fallen men and did his best to imitate Thor's voice. "You are not worthy."

Diana nodded in satisfaction. "Good work, people. Now, make sure we have pictures of each of these chuckleheads."

She focused her glasses on the nearest one and tapped the frame to take a still photo. The techs would already have video recordings of the flight from each of their display devices, but it nevertheless made sense to capture in the highest clarity where possible.

Then, considering their situation for a moment, she

added, "Take anything from them that seems useful. Same with the ones on the other side. Never can tell when we're going to need supplies."

Deacon had remained quiet through most of the fight. Now he chuckled over the comm. "That's right, people. Loot your kills."

Kayleigh added, "Khajit has wares if you have coin."

The infomancer laughed. "Excellent Skyrim impression."

Kayleigh replied, "I've got mad skills."

Rath and Max had rejoined Diana by this time. She looked down at her partner, shook her head, and rolled her eyes. He grinned. "Having fun is good."

She nodded. "Too true, buddy. I guess you gotta find it where you can get it, right?"

"Now you're thinking like a troll. You've evolved."

Diana laughed and went to gather the fallen rifles. If nothing else, the anti-magic bullets would make collecting them worth the effort.

CHAPTER NINE

K evin Serrano rose as Tash walked over to the table, then sat again as she did the same. He'd invited his second-in-command out for a fancy dinner at a local steakhouse, and the gesture was appropriate given the setting. They both fully understood it wasn't a date. *But when in Rome, one does what the Romans do.*

The change of environment was an effort to help him break out of thought processes that weren't serving him well, most notably the anger and exasperation he couldn't release over his rental mercenaries' failure to capture or kill any of Sheen's team.

Tash grinned as she set her napkin on her lap. She'd chosen to wear a business suit with a skirt, also entirely appropriate for the venue. He had on his suit, including a tie, again trying to separate the Kevin of this moment from the one who'd watched the dismal failure from his office's operations center.

His companion observed, "I always know when you

invite me out for an expensive meal that you're angry about something. Not hard to imagine what, this time."

He nodded but held off replying while he ordered his food. Tash did the same, adding a bottle of wine, and the tuxedoed server departed. Kevin replied, "I'm getting over it. Slowly. Sometimes it sucks having competent enemies."

She shrugged. "True. But without them, we'd be out of a job since *anyone* can take down idiots."

Kevin scowled. "I'm not sure Bradford's people would've managed to succeed even against idiots."

"I have to agree that it wasn't the most impressive display of martial prowess. What do you think went wrong?"

"You saw it, as I did. Outmatched from the beginning. Whatever team Bradford thought he was putting together, he oversold it. To us, at least. Maybe to himself, as well."

"I'm guessing both."

He gave a sharp nod. "Me too."

The server reappeared with a bottle of wine and offered it for the customary taste. Kevin deferred to Tash, whose knowledge was far better than his. *Although, when it comes to beer, she can't hold a candle to me.*

She pronounced it acceptable, and the waiter poured. A moment later, jumbo shrimp in cocktail sauce presented in a rocks glass appeared in front of each of them. When the man left, Kevin said, "Okay. Tell me your perspective on the fight and what conclusions you've drawn from it."

She chewed, swallowed, and patted her subtly painted lips with a napkin. "First, Sheen and her team are still playing by the big rule. They could've handled the situation a lot easier and with much less risk to themselves if they were willing to kill people. So, huge advantage for us."

Kevin sipped his wine, then again when he realized how good it tasted. He lifted it in a small salute to her selection before he set it back down. "Agreed. Nothing like a potential murder rap to entice you to consider alternate options."

"Right? Second, they brought an effective blend of magic and weaponry to bear. They're not as under-supplied as we'd hoped they'd be after we knocked out their base."

He sighed. "Yeah, I noticed that, too. They must've gotten away with some good stuff during their counterat-tack. Still, I doubt that's all of it. They have additional support from somewhere."

Tash gestured with her fork. "That was my conclusion as well. Still, we're keeping an eye on all the other ARES bureaus, and as far as I know, there's no evidence of anyone there helping her out."

"Sheen's too smart for that. She knows we'd be looking at them and wouldn't want to put others from that organi-zation in danger. No, it's probably someone else. Maybe in one of the kemanas."

"I could take a look."

Kevin shook his head. "While I know your bloodlines mean you're allowed to visit, I don't think you'd be all that welcome if anyone knew who you were. The rules down below are flexible enough that you might not come back."

She frowned and responded darkly, "I can handle myself."

"If we reversed the situation, would you let me do it?"

Tash sighed. "No. You're too valuable to risk."

"As are you, unless it's completely vital. So, what else?" Their shrimp cocktails vanished, and salads replaced them —the classic wedge, a large green triangle with bleu cheese, bacon, and a few other unique touches. He carved into his with a knife, trying not to think violent thoughts.

She said, "Overall, the mercs fought well, I guess. Against humans, they would've been effective. But neither they nor their magical support are in the highest echelon."

He chuckled. "That's because we have all the top people on our team."

She rolled her eyes. "Flatterer. Won't work on me."

"I know." Once upon a time, he'd considered making a romantic move on her, but it never seemed right. He was sure she felt the same—about the "not right" part, at least. He wouldn't delude himself into thinking she found him interesting in that way.

"I'd guess that lack of quality is why they were available. Given the government's need to handle hotspots world-wide, they've already deployed most of the best. Still, you're not wrong. They're not as skilled as our people and hopefully nowhere near as good as the squads that Nance and Leland are putting together."

She tapped her knife against her plate. "You know, the other thing about that group, their allegedly 'seamless' use of magicals wasn't seamless at all. Using them for shields? That's thinking small and stupid."

He pushed aside his salad plate, now free of food. "I thought the same thing. He's limiting himself with that arrangement. My guess is he still doesn't fully trust them."

"Because he's an anti-magical racist."

"Noted. It does you credit that you're not crowing with delight over his team's failure."

She tapped her chest and solemnly responded, "Inside, I am."

Kevin laughed. "No, you're not." His dinner arrived, a filet with sides of asparagus, creamed spinach, and a perfectly baked potato with butter and sour cream.

They talked of other things while they ate but came back to their battle debrief before dessert. He said, "So, Sheen and company swallowed the bait we fed them, and the mercenaries failed us. We'll need to have a chat with Bradford about that."

She grinned. "Oh, please, let me be the one to do it."

He matched her expression. "Maybe not, this time. Something tells me you might not be able to restrain yourself from throwing some insults his way."

"You know me well."

"In addition to discussing the situation with him, I think we should see how our other allies are coming along. Let's drop in for a visit with our Army friends."

Tash frowned at that idea. "In Colorado, you mean?" He nodded, and she lifted an eyebrow. "I'm guessing unannounced visitors to their supersecret base would piss them off."

He smiled. "Yep."

She tilted her head. "So, you're going to do that why?"

Kevin chuckled. "Not me. *We.* The fact is, they seem to have some confusion over where the power lies in our relationship. I think it's time we demonstrated that they're not on the top level of this particular food chain."

CHAPTER TEN

The cabin she shared with Deacon didn't offer much space for anything other than their computer setups. He'd helped her take the one empty corner and convert it into a tiny electronics shop, with crates full of equipment on the floor and enough counter area to get a little work done. At the moment, she was considering Diana's question of whether it was possible to redesign the power feed for the shock gloves to accommodate a second battery.

Kayleigh muttered, "I mean, it's obviously *possible*. The question lies in the failure point we'd add. There will have to be a junction unless I do two separate and parallel tracks, one battery to each glove." Her eyebrows drew together in a frown. "That's the easiest way. But you'll complain about it because it requires more cabling in the suit, and you're a whiner."

She reached over to the nearby laptop, which was running a design program, and put her two visions for the solution side-by-side. Further contemplation was interrupted by a *beeping* over her comm that indicated someone had appeared in their portal receiving room.

The tech wasn't wearing her display glasses at the moment, so she tapped the button on her laptop to show the camera feed. Ruby Achera waved up at the camera. She had a backpack over her shoulder. Kayleigh grinned, hit the command to unlock the landing room's exit, and headed out to meet her.

They met where the path from the receiving room and the one from her workshop converged on the way to the main building. Ruby said, "Hiya, K. What's up?"

"Trying to make the impossible possible for the boss, like usual. She has no sense of reality, I tell you."

Their guest laughed. A moment later, Rath scampered up to them with Max at his side. Kyleigh had informed the troll of Ruby's arrival. The Mist Elf offered a chest-high fist bump, and Rath leapt in the air and tapped it. Then Max reared back and reached up with his front paws to touch her fist as well. Ruby laughed again, and Kayleigh grinned. The troll said, "Good boy, Maxie."

Kayleigh reached down and ruffled his hair. "The *best* boy."

Rath asked, "No Idryll?"

Ruby shook her head. "First, since I would like to get some work done while I'm here, not bringing her was the logical choice. Second, she's sleeping. As usual."

Rath and Kayleigh laughed. She replied, "You can tell her other form is a cat."

The other woman nodded. "No question about it. So, do you want to see what I've brought you?"

Rath shouted, "Yes, yes, yes," and ran off toward the

main building. The women followed at a more sedate pace, talking and laughing as they walked.

Kayleigh liked Ruby, a technomancer who blended magic and technology in interesting ways. Kayleigh didn't have the magical ability, but she did have copious tech knowledge and partnered with Deacon to accomplish similar work. She'd never lacked for conversation topics with the other woman.

Ruby said, "It must be nice to have your boyfriend here with you finally."

She nodded. "Nice some of the time, sure. Downright annoying the rest of the time."

The Mist Elf laughed. "So, a typical boyfriend, then."

"Exactly. How's yours?"

"Complaining about how much time I'm spending on Oriceran. To be fair, it's a lot. So, on the one hand, it's good that he misses me. On the other, acting like a whiny toddler isn't particularly sexy, you know?"

Kayleigh snorted. "I dare you to say that to his face."

"Oh, hell no. There would be *more* whining."

They were still laughing as they entered the main building. Each claimed a seat around a large table, including Max, who sat on a chair beside Rath. Ruby pulled a plastic case about the size of a laptop but twice as thick from her backpack and opened the top. Nestled inside were blue crystals with a metal base encasing one end.

Rath asked, "Communication crystals? For the Network?"

Ruby nodded. "You guessed it. I'll help you attune them before I leave. That brings up an important question. Do you want them all attuned to one another? Or all attuned to one you can use as a hub? The first gives you flexibility, the second, control."

Kayleigh replied, "We'll go with the bottleneck model for now. I'd like to think that someday we could trust that everyone involved would be able to work together. Since it's new, maintaining centralized control makes a lot of sense."

Rath challenged, "Chicken."

She scowled. They'd had this argument several times, and she knew the troll understood the reasoning. Nonetheless, he persisted in claiming she was afraid. "Shut it, short stuff." He laughed.

Ruby set the crystals out on the table. "I think that's a good choice. So, tell me what you want to happen when one of your contacts sends in a signal."

Kayleigh replied, "Two things. First, a human will hear it, whoever's on duty at that moment. We'll rotate the task among the team members who are here at the base. That's so we can keep an ear out for trouble and intervene faster if it's an emergency. The main flow will go through an AI. Deacon and I are still tweaking that."

Ruby nodded. "So, you'll need to change the signal from magic to information a computer can use. The technological piece can do that. And then?"

"We'll want the AI to be able to send it out to the full network if needed, either automatically or after seeking permission, according to the ruleset we give it."

"So. From magic to information, then from information back to magic. I brought along the pieces you'll need. I can show you how to work them, and I'll send you the 3D printer specs to create them."

Kayleigh grinned, surprised. "Really? I didn't think you'd handled that for us."

Ruby nodded. "It was part of another project I was working on." She pulled out a smaller case from her backpack. Opening it revealed several additional crystals, each visible through a transparent window on a black metal cylinder.

"These will interface with your comms. They attach to the wireless base station everyone wears. If for any reason a clear signal from the electronics is lost, jamming or whatever, they'll seamlessly switch over to using magic to send signals until the other is viable again. We're keeping magic as a backup, so the crystals' power lasts longer."

Kayleigh replied, "Excellent. You're a gem."

Rath laughed. "A Ruby, even."

The Mist Elf reached into the bag, drew out another container, and opened it to show a bunch of discs stacked inside. "Replacement grenades, plus some EMPs. And finally, these." From the pouch on the front of the backpack, she produced a double handful of potion capsules attached to dermal pads, the kind they all wore under their clothes for instant access to healing or energy.

Kayleigh picked one up and turned it over in her hands. "This looks way more industrial than the last batch."

Ruby nodded. "We have an automated assembly process running now, funded by the wealthy magicals we'd originally and successfully imagined as the primary audience for the things.

"Turns out we were right about the demand. My father is *very* excited about the profit margin, enough so that we're using a quarter of the net to create extra packs to donate to magicals in law enforcement. Including you all."

She laughed. "Of course, I'm sure he plans to give them a taste now and start charging for them later. Savvy businesspeople, my parents."

Kayleigh shook her head. "Owning a successful casino isn't enough, huh?"

"Nothing will ever be enough for him. He lives for the game."

"You and Margrave come up with any other ideas for nonlethal stuff? I have to admit. I'm more or less at the end of my rope on that topic."

Ruby closed her bag. "An idea, but not ready to prototype yet. But what if we took the grenade canisters you're using for your launchers and modified them to attach to a drone? Then you would have some bots with nonlethal offensive capability. Send them in ahead of your people, hose down the area before you enter. Seems safer."

Rath clapped. "Plus caltrops."

Ruby grinned. "Of course, caltrops are standard drone equipment nowadays."

Kayleigh chuckled. The idea of drone-deployed spiked munitions to discourage pursuit had been the troll's, and it was a good one. "Excellent. I can't thank you enough, Ruby. None of us can."

The other woman nodded, then her expression shifted to concern. "Any news about Bryant?"

She sighed. She knew how awful she'd feel if anyone captured Deacon. She was sure Diana felt worse since she doubtless blamed herself for not being able to see into the future and prevent it.

"None. We're going to have to go all-out in D.C. Deacon's getting ready right now for an attack on some systems we shouldn't be in, according to him. I've never seen him worry this much about a run, so I think he's probably not exaggerating. Still, it doesn't look like Serrano is leaving us a choice."

"If you need me, Idryll, and Morrigan, say the word and we're there."

She managed a smile. "I'll let the boss know. We're not too proud to turn down help at this particular moment."

Ruby rose and threw her backpack over her shoulder. "Good. If there's one thing I've learned as leader of the Mist Elves, it's that we're strongest when we work together."

Rath nodded and said with all the confidence in the world, "That's why we're going to win."

CHAPTER ELEVEN

Rath stood on top of the cathedral, peering out at the twinkling lights of the Oakland suburb to the east of Pittsburgh. Even though darkness was falling, the university campus was still active, with people scurrying to and fro wrapped in thick coats against the cold. Laughter occasionally reached his perch's lofty height. *Too bad it didn't snow. Snow would've been nice.*

He thought back to when the team's base was in the city and the friends he'd made during that part of his life. He looked forward to renewing a couple of those acquaintances tonight.

It had been an enjoyable time, all things considered, even with the dangers they faced. He'd left the city a very different troll than he'd entered it and would always have fond memories of that time. *But now, I have responsibilities to take care of.*

He said, "Gwen, air currents, please."

The female voice of his AI replied, "Of course."

He threw himself off the edge of the building, forty-some stories up, and his flight suit wings snapped out to full extension. They caught the updraft, represented as a series of red lines in his display, which buffeted him upward. He moved from one scarlet zone to the next, gliding in a general circle around the tall tower for no reason other than the pure joy of flying. Time didn't permit more than one rotation, unfortunately.

"Gwen, give me a path." Golden diamonds in a long line appeared in his visual field, lines creating that shape around empty spaces, serving as markers for him to fly through.

He banked in the proper direction and passed into the first, and Gwen played a small video game sound in his ears. He laughed, then laughed more as a numerical score appeared on his display. All the AIs' personalities seemed to be changing and developing faster lately as if they'd crossed a threshold of some kind, and he was absolutely in favor of it.

He steered through each designated waypoint, occasionally staying straight, sometimes banking through them, and once or twice performing a barrel roll. He discovered that as long as he didn't screw up and sacrifice more altitude than expected, he got bonus points for acrobatics. A grin stretched his lips as he flew. His uniform kept him warm, and while the wind chafed the parts of his face that the goggles didn't cover, it wasn't enough of a distraction to take away from the joy of flight.

He noticed familiar territory below. "Gwen, please create a waypoint for Chan." A new set of diamonds appeared in green rather than yellow, and he banked left to soar through the nearest.

Rath fondly remembered the man who'd taught him to throw knives, the memory always nearby given how often the troll employed the skills he'd learned under his tutelage. Unfortunately, the flight over his former training space revealed nothing useful, and he made a mental note to check in on Chan at his first opportunity. He rejoined the yellow diamonds and steered toward his target.

He landed in the back yard, touching down in a pool of darkness on the boundary between houses. His wings retracted seamlessly into the rectangular container on his back, and he remained still while his goggles scanned the house. Only two heat signatures were present within the home, which fit with what Kayleigh's drone had observed during its surveillance of the place.

Emmanuel and Professor Charlotte were living there together now, it appeared. The fact that changes had occurred in this corner of his life while he was away was a source of some irritation. He wanted everything to remain pristine, as it was in his memory, a favorite movie he could revisit anytime he liked.

Of course, reality wasn't like that. People had to grow and change. He laughed, thinking about how those words applied to him on so many levels and allowed the momentary negativity to fall away.

Rath stayed in the shadows as much as possible as he made his way to the back door. He knocked, then stood away from it so they wouldn't feel threatened by someone standing in the doorway. *Plus, if they look through the peephole, I might not be tall enough for them to see me.*

Professor Charlotte opened the door with a broad smile on her face. If anything, Manny's grin under his silver-shot beard was even wider from his position behind her. They let him in, and the gray-haired woman dropped to one knee, wrapping him in a hug that made the dangly earrings she always wore sway with the motion. "Rath. It's been so long. We missed you."

He nodded, and when she released him, he traded a fist bump with Manny. "Been busy. Wanted to get back but couldn't. Apologies."

She laughed and rose to her feet. "None necessary. But if I'd known you were coming, I would've had something prepared."

Manny said, "Those cookies are in the freezer."

Charlotte smiled. "But *surely* Rath isn't interested in fresh-baked cookies."

He laughed. "I could be."

"Got twenty minutes?"

"Definitely. I need to talk to you about something, after. Cookies first."

They spent those twenty minutes chatting about nothing in particular, then sat together at the dining room table, each with a cup of tea and a small plate with three cookies. A larger plate with another dozen or so of them rested in the middle of the polished wooden surface. Rath took a bite of one and sighed happily. "Chocolate chip. So good."

Manny said, "You know you can come by anytime for a snack, buddy."

He nodded and turned reluctantly to current events. "We had to leave our base."

Charlotte said softly, "I saw your friends' pictures on

the news. We didn't believe what they said about them, of course. We know you too well for that."

Rath frowned at the reminder that the media was representing them as criminals, at best. "Challenging times. The rules were stupid, so we didn't follow them. Must have made someone mad."

She snorted. "Yeah, people are like that. I usually find myself on the other side of that equation with my students, though."

Manny said, "I'd love to think you're only here for a social call, my friend, but that seems unlikely given all that's going on. Are you on the trail of Rhazdon artifacts again?"

Rath lifted a hand and waggled it back and forth. "Sort of. Artifacts involved. Here for two things. First, heard anything about a magical cult? Maybe artifact-related?"

The pair exchanged glances, then Manny replied, "Yes. Charlotte, I, and some new associates have handled a few low-level problems with magicals here in town since you left. Basically, people behaved badly and needed a smack upside the head. Figuratively, of course."

Rath grinned. "If not figurative, you give me a call." He punched a hand into an open palm, and his friends laughed.

Charlotte added, "While doing so, we've heard rumors about an organized magical religious group working out of an old, abandoned church on the river northwest of the city. That might be what you're talking about. I'm not sure it has anything to do with artifacts."

Rath replied, "Worth checking out, anyway. Thank you. The other reason for my visit is this." He detached a small black pouch from his belt, laid it on the table, and opened it. Four crystals nestled within, the new communication devices Ruby had provided.

He explained, "They work with magic or only technology. Allows you to send us a message. We're building a network of people so we can all stay informed of things. A rumor in Pittsburgh, rumor in New Orleans, rumor in Las Vegas, suddenly no longer a rumor but something to investigate."

They nodded and took the crystals. Charlotte asked, "Shouldn't you all be hiding out rather than trying to do stuff like this?"

He shrugged. "Those who can do, must do." He gestured at the crystals. "You should put them inside something. Hide them. Don't want them falling into the wrong hands."

Manny held his up toward the chandelier that hung over the table, turning it to get a look at all sides. He asked, "Who does it connect to? You?"

"One of us will always be listening, and there's an AI, too. Maybe Harley or Alfred. Messages will come to you when needed. So, keep it around."

Charlotte asked, "Why this, and not something like phones or Internet?"

Rath replied, "Government can monitor those things. Can't listen in on this."

Manny spoke in a gentle tone. "Your team feels betrayed, I bet." The troll gave a small nod, and he continued, "I would, too. Totally understandable that you'd want something that would go past them given that they've turned on you."

Charlotte nodded her agreement. "You don't have to worry. No one will know you were here."

Rath grinned. "Thanks. More cookies?"

She laughed and slid another trio onto his plate. "Of course."

After munching for a bit, he asked, "Know good people in other cities?"

Charlotte and Manny exchanged glances and said a couple of names to each other, quickly agreeing on a pair of people they trusted. Rath nodded and repeated them, instructing Gwen to record them. "Excellent. We'll check them out, maybe add them to the Network."

Many laughed. "The Network. It sounds very fancy."

"Needs a better name. Still working on it."

Charlotte grinned. "I'm sure you'll come up with something good. In the meantime, let me catch you up on what's been going on here in town. So much has changed."

Rath spent the next hour laughing, joking, and generally enjoying himself with his two friends. Finally, though, he apologized and told them it was time for him to leave. "Have someone else to visit." *Hopefully, he won't keep his promise to kill me if I visit him again.*

CHAPTER TWELVE

Rath glided over the cemetery, noting that little had changed since his last visit. He very much hoped the same would be true at his destination.

He dipped into a descent on the far side of the graveyard, landing near a culvert protruding from the hillside. It was slick with icy water down the center, and the metal skin radiated cold. He knew traps awaited him inside because the man he sought had told him there would be and because he'd been down that path before. *But I bet the traps will be all new.*

The person whose lair rested inside the culvert had also informed Rath that if the troll ever violated his sanctuary again, the response would most likely be fatal. *Assuming I survive the traps in the first place.*

Still, he had no other way to find Amadeo, and the idea that the assassin could be a useful resource for Diana and the rest of the team wouldn't leave his brain no matter how often he shooed it away. *If nothing else, he's good at hiding.*

Maybe has tips to share. Who knows how long we'll be doing this? Might need them.

He pulled off his flight gear and hid it in a cluster of low evergreen bushes near the culvert. Setting his goggles to detect heat signatures, he turned a slow circle, ensuring no one was watching him from nearby. He spotted a rabbit and a squirrel, but nothing more dangerous than that. Satisfied, he shifted the glasses back into multi-sensor mode, customizing the view to leave one lens clear while the other showed an overlay of the detection scans.

The last time he'd visited this place, the traps along the way had been primarily physical, but he wasn't about to assume that would be the case again. He checked to be sure his knives were ready to be drawn and tapped the hilts of his batons to ensure they were where they were supposed to be. They were, of course. *Stop stalling, stupid.*

He pulled the grate that covered the opening away and entered, maintaining his three-foot size. It was adequate to walk with his feet on either side of the icy center. The first trap was positioned only a short distance in—a tripwire placed a third of the way up from the floor. He followed it back to the walls and discovered a hook anchored it on one side. It disappeared into a small box on the other, probably containing explosives or something even nastier.

The logical inclination would be to step over the wire. However, the assassin was extremely crafty, and since he would've known that was a natural choice, Rath froze and looked carefully in all directions.

The slight glint of glass revealed an electric eye and his scan showed the infrared beam cutting across two-thirds of the way up toward the cylinder's ceiling. He could shrink down to his smallest form and avoid both easily, but he'd have to leave his weapons and gear behind to do it. That was an unacceptable option given the mystery of what lay ahead.

Instead, he stayed low and stepped over the tripwire, careful not to let his spiky hair break the infrared beam. He managed a few more steps before the feeling of imminent danger came to him again, and he stopped moving. Rath didn't think the place would be equipped with sound-based defenses because they would be too easy to trigger accidentally. Physical traps were his primary concern, along with things like the infrared beam from before.

He spotted another sensor, and because it didn't have a beam associated with it, judged it was probably a motion detector. Gwen gave him an image of the most likely detection zone for the trap, and he carefully avoided that area as he advanced as slowly as possible past it.

Part of him was starting to think that coming back to this place was a bad idea, but now that he was this far in, it seemed stupid to give up. He recognized that thinking for the fallacy it was but kept going anyway. *This could make a difference.*

He found another tripwire, and while stepping over, detected a pressure plate as he was about to lower his foot onto it. Only its slightly different texture from the rest of the surrounding metal gave it away. He was even more careful after that, losing track of time and thinking of nothing but the need to make it safely through the culvert.

Finally, he reached a familiar intersection guarded by a locked door. His electrical display showed the location of the sensor pad inside the wall, and the small computer lock pick he carried defeated it in less than a minute. He cringed at the thought of what would've happened if it had been unable to do so. *Boom, baby.*

He pulled the door open carefully and stepped through. The underground chamber was as he remembered it, a mausoleum without any coffins inside. *Abandoned by the family, or something like that, Amadeo said.* Stairs on one side led up to the exit into the graveyard, which was doubtless as heavily trapped as the back way had been. He idly wondered how Amadeo disarmed the traps when he used the entrances and exits or if he did the same careful navigation Rath had done. *Somehow, I doubt it.*

When he'd been here last, the place had been clean, and some gear had been unpacked and assembled. Now it looked deserted. Equipment crates were still present, each with its electronic and physical locks. *Keeping it as a supply dump, at least.*

Dust was everywhere, enough that it made his nose itch as his footsteps propelled the stuff into the air. Rath scowled, his spirits dipping in the face of the assassin's absence. "I know it was a lot to ask, but it would've been nice of you to be here so I could talk to you."

He paused, thinking that in a movie this would be the point where some slumbering system woke up and talked back to him, one that had lain dormant while waiting for the hero to arrive. Nothing happened. He muttered, "Life should be more like the movies."

Then he began a methodical search of the room in case Amadeo had left behind a note or some other clue. He completed his circuit without finding a lead and growled in frustration. *Well, at least I got the crystals to Manny and Professor Charlotte. That's something. Not a total waste.*

He turned to leave, trying to recapture his concentration for the trap-filled exit, and his eye caught a detail he hadn't registered before. He walked over to it and realized that what he'd initially taken for a simple crack in the wall was carved there, an image deliberately chipped out of the stone. More, it bore a striking resemblance to a stylized version of his hair, a continuous line showing the individual pieces sticking up all over the place.

His heartbeat sped up a little as he realized the assassin might've left a message behind for him after all. He pushed on the line, but it had no effect. He looked up, to the left, then the right, but noticed nothing unusual there, either.

Finally, his head tilted down, where a low gap was present in the stone wall. The opening was too small and narrow for a human to fit their hand in, but not so minuscule he couldn't crawl into it at his smallest size.

He quickly removed his gear, shivering in the cold as the base layer came off, then crawled through the hole. The inside was dark, as the whole mausoleum had been. Without his goggles' night vision, he couldn't see a thing. He *felt* something, though—cold, plastic and metal, and rectangular. It was barely small enough that he could shove it out through the opening. He did so and followed it, then grew back to normal size, put his goggles on, and looked at it.

The tiny device with a hinge at the top had a logo from a major cell phone company. He dressed again, shivering once in a mixture of pain and pleasure as the heating function of his uniform kicked in. Then he lifted what was clearly a flip phone and held it at arm's length to open it, still wary of the potential for a trap. Nothing happened, so he pushed the power button.

The same logo appeared on the tiny black-and-white screen above the numbers, then disappeared. It was replaced by the words **Press # four times. Wait.**

He momentarily wondered whether doing so would be a bad idea, perhaps triggering yet another trap, but shrugged away the worry. He'd come here to get in touch with Amadeo, and it seemed as if the assassin had left him, and *only* him, a method to do so.

He followed the instructions and looked at the screen expectantly. After five minutes of nothingness, he powered off the phone and put it in a belt pouch. *Maybe it takes a while for the message to reach him. Anyway, time for me to get home.* He grinned as he walked back toward the door, thinking that the night had turned out to be a definite success, even if it hadn't exactly gone as he'd hoped.

CHAPTER THIRTEEN

Cara was on duty when the team received its first message over the new communication system. The Network acted more like voicemail than a real-time back and forth. It sent the message as a whole rather than word by word. She supposed they'd eventually get used to the slight delay involved to use it for regular conversation, but it worked, and the content was important enough that it sent her looking for Diana.

She found the boss in the training area, whipping through sword forms with Fury in her hands, her speed boosted by an expenditure of magic. After watching her hack and slash several imaginary opponents to presumed death, Cara called, "Don't kill me. I surrender."

Diana leapt in the air and performed a spinning strike, ending it with her sword extended in a lunge accompanied by a loud shout. Then she sheathed the weapon, grabbed a nearby cloth to wipe the sweat from her face, and walked over. "What's up, woman?"

She laughed. "Got a message over the Network from Zeb. Says we should come down for a chat tonight."

Diana shook her head. "I'll pass on that one. I need to keep looking for something that will lead us to Bryant. It's all yours."

Pursuing clues to find their missing member had been the other woman's only occupation since he'd vanished. Frankly, Cara had been surprised to find her working out instead of in the techs' workspace, hovering and demanding answers. *Positive sign. At least for Kayleigh and Deacon.* "Okay, I'll take care of it. I'll put Rath on Network oversight."

Diana chuckled. "He'll be thrilled. Maybe have Zeb call him for kicks."

"Will do."

The levity left her friend's face. "Keep your comm on, though. If we get a lead, I'll need you here regardless of what's going on down there. Bryant is our only priority right now."

Cara nodded. "Got it, boss."

At ten o'clock in the evening local time, Cara portaled into the basement of the Drunken Dragons tavern, appearing among the clutter of crates, boxes, and kegs. She'd chosen boots, jeans, a T-shirt, and her favorite leather jacket to blend in with the crowd. They probably wouldn't be carrying *quite* as many hidden weapons, but on the surface, she looked like simply another person out for a night on the town. *Where better to do that than New Orleans?*

Zeb was busy serving when she arrived, so she wandered to a spot next to where he'd deposit drinks for delivery onto the main floor. The place was hopping. Its three long tables were mostly full, and there were no seats left at the bar.

A strange snort came from nearby, and she levered herself up on her tiptoes to look over the edge of the bar. A reptilian form lay behind it, curled up on the floor, and she broke into a grin as she realized who it was. "Fyre, buddy, long time no see."

The draksa, a dragon-like creature the size of a large dog, lifted an eyelid, regarded her with a hint of a smile, and closed it again. Cara turned to survey the tavern's main room. Sure enough, Zeb had an extra server out there taking care of his patrons. Her striking red hair was obvious as she made her way across the tavern floor, trading insults and jibes with the customers as she threaded through them toward the bar.

The dwarf came over, and Cara asked, "Did you invite me down to say hi to Cali? If so, thanks. I should've brought Rath, though. He'll be sad to have missed the chance to wrestle with Fyre."

Zeb chuckled. The dwarf's blue eyes met hers as he shook his head, pulling softly on his long black beard. "Nope, not only a social call. Got some news about that religious bunch you're after. First, what will you have?"

"You pick for me." It was the only appropriate answer to that question in this place. Zeb nodded approval and headed for the cask resting on the far side of the long bar, near the door. It held the ever-changing house special brew. When he returned, it was with a red-tinted lager that tasted even better than it looked, which was saying something.

Cali bustled up, set her tray on the bar's surface, and yelled a set of orders to Zeb. He scowled. "Hold your horses."

The redhead imitated his voice perfectly. "Get yours moving, old man." She turned to Cara and wrapped her in a hug.

She laughed and patted the young woman on the back. When Cali released her, Cara asked, "How are things in New Atlantis?"

Cali offered a quick shrug. "Same old, same old. Spending my time making sure my family's secure from whatever challenge someone gets it in their mind to throw at us next."

Cara nodded. She didn't understand all the rules of the combative and competitive society that existed in New Atlantis but knew it occasionally proved an annoyance to Cali. *Of course, it also allowed her to gain some serious power down there, which is a reasonable offset for the irritation.*

She'd been kind of hoping their work would take them to the undersea city again, but thus far, the team's efforts had stayed limited to places above the water. "So why the visit?"

"Well, mainly, Zeb thinks I owe him for all he did for me." She rolled her eyes. "So, once in a while, I show up to play into his delusions."

From across the bar, the dwarf shouted, "I heard that."

Cali called, "Shouldn't you be making drinks? Some of our customers would like to get home before tomorrow." She continued in a lower voice, "He mentioned that you'd encountered a cult connected to Rhazdon artifacts. I thought you should know they have a presence in New Atlantis, too."

Cara frowned. "Really? It seems like a tough place to break into, you know? Did it start there?"

Cali shrugged. "I couldn't say. Obviously, we have a connection to Rhazdon since they were half-Atlantean. At the very least, one of the noble families is acting as a patron to the group there."

Cara's frown deepened. "Is that something to worry about? Do you need help?"

Cali shook her head, making her scarlet ponytail swing. "No. If necessary, I can challenge them. They don't have many good fighters so it wouldn't be all that much of a risk. I doubt the family members themselves are believers. They like causing trouble. I guess that's true of most of the noble families, come to think of it."

Cara laughed. "But not yours, of course."

Cali grinned wide. "Oh, *hell* no. We Leblancs live to cause trouble."

Zeb put six drinks down on her tray. "Got that right, missy."

Cali retorted, "Bite me, bristle beard."

He snarled, "Move your ass, serving girl," and she left with a laugh. Zeb smiled with a hint of regret. "Not the same without her here."

Cara nodded. "I can imagine. So, you mentioned some news?"

"Yeah. The group you hit here doesn't seem to have been particularly bothered by it, at least according to the rumors I hear. Apparently, they changed location and kept on keeping on. They've supposedly taken over an abandoned building in an office park."

"A lot of those around still, huh?"

"True. Hurricanes suck. Anyway, you wouldn't know they were there except that some of their people come to town to find new followers. They play it off like they're telling stories about voodoo, but if someone seems interested, they switch to trying to recruit them."

She frowned. "That's a lot of detail for a rumor."

He scratched his chin under his beard. "I might've gone out and done some reconnaissance. You know, to check things out a little."

"That's much appreciated. Anything else?"

His expression turned angry, and she got a hint of what it must've been like to face him during his time as a warrior. He growled, "Yeah. More people going missing than usual. Mostly magicals."

Cara scowled at the implications. "Think they're recruiting them?"

He shrugged. "Could be. No way to tell. Based on what you said about the whole sacrifice thing, it seems as if it might be worth investigating."

CHAPTER FOURTEEN

Tash had used some contacts from outside the team to get them a portal to Colorado. Now Kevin was behind the wheel of a rental sedan, headed for the hidden facility in the Rocky Mountain Arsenal wildlife refuge. He was sure that Major Leland and Colonel Nance would be annoyed at their unexpected visit. He couldn't bring himself to care.

It came down to the fact that he had permission to be on the base by virtue of his team's interactions with the Army. Despite the clear signals from the officers that he wasn't welcome in their playground, they had no real means to stop him from exercising that privilege.

Tash had questioned the decision several times, as a good second-in-command should do. Kevin knew it would cause some immediate trouble. Still, his sights were set on putting eyeballs on the team and hopefully pulling them into the field, whether they were fully ready to the Army's standards or not. *They can't do much worse than the mercenaries, that's for sure.*

He'd flipped the order of their contacts from his initial plan, deferring the conversation with Bradford indefinitely. The head of the defense contracting company had left a voicemail, but Kevin was content to let him stew for a while. *Allow the failure to sink in. That should make you more receptive to suggestions. I bet Tash has a ton.*

Laughing inwardly, he looked across at his passenger and found her staring at him. "What?"

She shook her head. "You've been quiet for, like, fifteen minutes but making faces the whole time. Clearly, you're arguing with someone in your brain. You cracking up on me, boss? Hearing voices?"

He gave a decisive nod. "Yes. One hundred percent. I've lost every single one of my marbles, and you should immediately put me out to pasture. Tahiti is nice, I hear."

Tash grinned. "People like us don't get retirements. We keep working until someone kills us or we fall over from natural causes."

He shook his head. "Bleak, Kline. Real bleak."

"Or maybe we get shot by the Army for showing up at their base despite entirely clear indications that they'd rather not have us there."

He turned the wheel, crossing the boundary into the refuge. "Those guys are jerks. I'm not saying that because they're Army. I've known lots of folks from all the military branches who are decent people, the kind you'd want at your side in a fight and the same position at the bar afterward. These two, they've got flag staffs shoved so far up their—"

Tash lifted a hand with a laugh. "Enough. We're close. They'll hear you somehow or sense your insult in the Force or something. Then we'll end up dead and buried in the desert."

"Technically, there's no desert nearby."

"They'll drive us to Nevada in a black Humvee."

He laughed. "You're not *that* against this mission, are you?"

She sighed and rolled her neck. "Part of me gets it. The other part of me thinks we have resources of our own that we haven't employed yet, and pushing the Army is still unnecessary."

"Meaning you and Makka."

"Of course."

He slowed the car to slightly under the speed limit, giving them a little extra time to finish this conversation before heading in. He wanted her mind to be clear and focused, and obviously, this was a long-standing issue for her.

"You know I don't doubt your abilities. The fact is, they magically outnumber us. Letting Sheen and her team have access to their magic during a battle so you could too only tilts the table to their advantage. If we could isolate Sheen, I'd send you in without reservation."

"But not Bates."

That was a question he held no doubts about. "Bates would've portaled away as fast as he could, and we would've lost him. Sheen, though, she'd stand and fight. It's who she is."

His partner blew out a breath. "Yeah, okay. I get it. That doesn't mean I have to like it. *Or* this crazy scheme of yours."

He laughed. "Hell, if you agreed with all the things I did,

you wouldn't be doing your job as my second. Now, time to put on our ultra-respectful military-interface faces."

She nodded and lifted a hand to her brow in a salute. "Aye, aye, Commodore."

He let out an unexpected snort. "Wrong branch."

"Sir, yes sir, Gunnery Sergeant."

"Marines. Getting closer."

She laughed and sang, "Over hill, over dale, we will hit the dusty trail, as the caissons go rolling along."

The song continued as he circled to the back of the buildings that were the only structures for miles around. The hidden ramp lowered in response to a signal from his ID tag. He'd gone past the major and the colonel to get the credentials loaded onto his identifier, which would irritate them to no end.

Still, in the words of one of his superiors from a long time before, he wasn't in it to make friends. *I'm in it to win it, and no obtuse military contingent is going to stop me.*

He hadn't been to the base before but had seen the files detailing it so the small underground pseudo-city wasn't a surprise. Careful review of the map had let him memorize the path in, and he drove straight to the training building. He parked outside and led Tash through the front door, which opened obediently to his ID. A check of the schedule board verified a session planned for that day, one with all three Army squads, exactly as their computer network had promised.

The officers would probably be additionally irritated to know he had access to that, too. In their places, he would be as well. Kevin had long before cultivated a contact high up in the Army's authority structure who now owed him several favors. As long as he kept his requests simple, he had no doubt they'd continue to be approved.

They found the training field, which held twelve magicals engaged in a three-way battle that looked alarmingly real.

Colonel Nance was present, his stiff-spined figure watching over the combat. Major Leland was as well, and he stomped toward them. When he got close, Kevin raised both hands.

"Peace, Major. You already know we have the authority to be here, and if for some bizarre reason you don't, feel free to verify it up your chain of command. We're not here to cause trouble, only to see how things are going and have a conversation about getting these guys into the field for real."

The officer scowled, but Kevin's words didn't leave him much room to object. He growled, "I *will* check. If anything's not on the level, I'll nail you to the wall."

He shrugged. "You're welcome to try. Until then, how about we play nice?"

They followed him to stand near Nance, who acknowledged them with a nod, but nothing more. The fight before them shifted and flowed with a sense of controlled chaos, the teams working as units to maximize their ability to attack and defend in the changing circumstances. Tash bumped her shoulder into his and muttered, "*That's* how you integrate magicals into a team."

"Not only protection bubbles. I get it. Although they're not really integrated since they're all magicals. One backpack and this is a very different scene."

"They're still Army. I bet they carry guns as well as wands or whatever."

"Let's hope."

A couple of minutes later, Major Leland called a halt and summoned one of the soldiers to their side. Colonel Nance said, "Stevens, your work has been flawless. I think it's time we recognized that effort."

The man, whose dark eyes matched the stubble of his crewcut, broke out in a grin. "Outstanding, sir."

Nance nodded. "Let's get you promoted then."

Kevin and Tash followed in silence as the group walked out of the facility to a building across the street. It notably lacked a plate signifying its purpose. They entered through a security door that scanned their ID cards, then had to present their credentials again twice more to humans to reach the inside.

Leland escorted the soldier into a medium-sized room while the rest of them stayed outside the doorway. Nance explained, "Isolation cell. It has several layers of walls, brick, metal, wood, stone, and more metal."

Tash replied, "Sounds safe. Like, King Kong safe."

The Army officer nodded. "That's its intent."

The three security doors that barricaded the chamber locked with loud sounds, and the major led them into a room filled with monitors. On each was a camera mounted inside the cell, showing Stevens from several angles. One technician sat behind a computer console, and Nance ordered, "Deploy the artifact."

Movement on one of the screens caught Kevin's attention as a silver metal box was lowered into the space. Stevens stood at parade rest in a corner, presumably instructed to do so, and stiffened as the box met the floor. The line that had delivered it retracted, and the sides of the container flipped down, revealing an object that looked like a lizard made of stone. It rushed immediately to the only other being in the cell and leapt on him. Stevens managed to keep his face neutral until the artifact burrowed into his arm, then fell to the ground and lay there twitching violently, his entire body shuddering.

Kevin asked, "They're fighting for control?"

The colonel nodded and flexed his fist. "It's not an easy battle, let me tell you."

After a minute, Stevens stopped trembling, rose smoothly to his feet, and saluted one of the cameras. "I have it subdued, sir. You can let me out."

Colonel Nance looked down at the tech, who had been monitoring data coming from the secure chamber. The man shook his head, and Nance ordered, "Put him out."

Clouds of gas billowed into the cell. Stevens screamed in rage, and tentacles boiled out of his arm to slam at the walls, floors, and exit door ineffectively. After several seconds, he went down to his knees and slumped to the floor.

Tash asked, "Voice analysis?"

Nance nodded. "For whatever reason, that's how we can best tell who's in control."

Kevin said, "This time, it was the artifact?"

"Affirmative. He'll have several more opportunities to master the thing. Hopefully, we'll find a way to help him succeed. If not, he'll die trying, and we'll put that artifact into secure storage as too powerful for use."

A chill ran through Kevin, even though it was exactly

how he would've done it if he were in charge. *They're all volunteers, after all. They knew what they were getting into. As much as anyone can with these damn artifacts, anyway.*

"So, while this was exceedingly educational, the real reason for my visit is that I've got a good line on where Sheen and her team might show up soon. Are you ready to put the rest of your people into the field for real?"

Nance gave him a rare smile. "Very much so."

CHAPTER FIFTEEN

An unaccustomed surge of nervousness flowed through Sloan as he entered the Senate building once again. *Knowing that people are trying to capture you and likely would have if they'd been a little better at their jobs can cause that, I imagine.* He shrugged it off. *I've been in difficult situations before, with far higher stakes. I've got this.*

His look was different enough that it fooled his team's image recognition scans, so he was confident it would do the same to any others attempting to identify him. He'd thinned his hair, giving himself widow's peaks and allowing a bit of his scalp to show through his swept-back style. It was a different color, as well, now dark brown with a hint of gray, with matching eyebrows.

This persona, unlike his other lobbyist incarnation, didn't have the money for expensive suits. He wore an off-the-rack tan one that didn't fit particularly well over a cream shirt with a light blue tie. His shoes were worn but serviceable and looked as if he'd attempted to give them at least some polish. "Taylor Kyrell" was also a lobbyist, but for much smaller industries, ones that wouldn't have the importance to secure a meeting with top-tier legislators.

He had appointments scheduled with the assistants to several senators, all of which would get canceled after he was already in the building. He wasn't looking to keep this persona running, so burning bridges wouldn't be a problem.

His illusion detection bracelet was back at the base, as was his normal watch with all its clever features. He still had some tricks on him, though, in his replacement watch, his belt, and the software loaded on his phone. It should be adequate for the day's mission, which was to get a listening device into the office of Senator Borowski from the great state of Nevada.

The Silver State, where everything is for sale. Including, probably, its politicians.

His character's lack of confidence was obvious in the way he walked, the way he held himself, and the slight nervousness with which he spoke. Sloan was good enough that he didn't have to concentrate on making any of those things happen. He simply held the idea of the character in his head, and it all flowed out naturally.

He glanced back after passing through security. His magical flash activated, telling him that the guard who'd checked him through had no suspicions, was extra tired today due to a late party the night previous, and looked eagerly forward to an anniversary dinner with his wife that weekend.

Sloan let the small smile that discovery evoked reach his lips as he walked down one of the corridors that led toward his supposed destination, the less impressive offices at the back of the building. Before he got there, he took several other turns, navigating the labyrinth created by frequent renovations to a door marked "Employees Only." As he neared it, he tapped a pattern on the top of his watch, instructing it to emit a jamming frequency for a moment to fuzz out the camera watching over the hallway.

The code-breaking software in his phone defeated the ID reader mounted beside the locked door. He pushed through quickly and closed it casually behind him. Inside was a room packed with lockers connected to another filled with janitorial and maintenance gear.

He opened several lockers until he found what he was looking for, one of the building staff's standard jumpsuits. He changed into it, including a footwear change into some work boots that didn't quite fit but were close enough that he'd still be able to use them without visible discomfort.

Sloan moved into the other room, snagged a radio and a headset from a shelf, and clipped it onto his jumpsuit's trouser pocket as he'd seen many others do. He also grabbed a toolbox, one with appropriate tools for electrical work, then messed up his perfect hair before heading out the door.

Even though he wore the same face as Kyrell, his body language differed as a member of the building's staff, channeling a certain annoyance mixed with a little subservience. He kept a plastic smile on his lips and nodded at security when he passed them, pretending to be in conversation with his superior over his headset. When people in suits and dresses approached, he moved to the side to let them pass, playing the role of worker bee among the bosses with ease. He stopped and pretended to check several things along his way, an ID panel here, an electrical box there.

It took him twenty minutes to finally arrive at his destination. Moving past the door and pretending to lace up his boot, he tapped another code onto the crown of his watch. This one would go out on an encrypted channel to Kayleigh, who would instruct their asset to move.

About a minute later, a woman emerged from the office. Borowski's administrative assistant headed toward the front. They'd arranged for a delivery to the senator that would require a signature. It was, in fact, a lovely gift basket, sent on behalf of a lobbying company she already worked with, one that would raise no alarms.

As soon as she was out of sight, Sloan used his phone to unlock the door and headed inside. The outer office looked very much like Richardson's assistant's, and the admin hadn't cleared her laptop screen. He'd come prepared with the right software on his phone to crack her password, but it turned out not to be necessary thanks to her quick response to the delivery.

He called up Borowski's schedule and discovered two important pieces of information. First, she wasn't in at the moment so he could plant the listening device directly in her office rather than in her assistant's area. That was the best possible outcome for the mission.

The second piece of news was even better. Borowski had a meeting scheduled with Richardson that afternoon, only a few hours away, and would be traveling to his office for it. Where they already had a bug.

He entered the senator's inner sanctum. Unlike Richardson's working space, it was strikingly devoid of personality. The requisite flags were in place at the corners of the room, and the bookshelves were full of the appropriately serious books, but they lacked personal touches and mementos.

Normally senators displayed framed pictures of themselves with important people, presidents, leaders, billionaires, that sort of thing. Borowski had none of that, only an impressive wooden desk supporting two laptops with a legal pad and fountain pen set beside them.

With no need for subtlety, he pushed her chair out and knelt to place the bug on the underside of the desk near the center, then headed back out. He passed the administrative assistant in the hallway. She was carrying an overly large fruit basket adorned with an ostentatious gold ribbon.

Sloan spent ten more minutes walking around pretending to be a maintenance worker, then headed back to the locker room. Someone else was inside when he arrived, so he took his time stowing his equipment and returning his radio to the charging station.

When the interloper departed, he changed into the clothes he'd entered the building in and headed for the exit. One more set of taps on his watch told Kayleigh to send in the next delivery, a mammoth bunch of brightly colored balloons, numerous enough to catch everyone's attention, including the guards'. The one watching the egress waved him through without looking at him too closely, which was precisely what he'd hoped for.

Sloan released a relieved breath as he exited the Senate building, then headed straight for the nearest taxi lane. His next stop would be an office complex across town where a small office rented under an assumed name allowed Sloan to portal back and forth from D.C. unnoticed. Once the car had pulled away from the curb, he sent a text message to Kayleigh.

B and R meeting at two. His office. Probably worth listening to.

He closed his eyes and relaxed, confident that he was safe and secure for at least as long as the ride lasted.

CHAPTER SIXTEEN

Diana wouldn't willingly miss a second of the meeting between Richardson and Borowski, so she and Cara had brought chairs into the techs' cabin from the main building to listen in reasonable comfort for as long as it lasted. As they positioned them between Kayleigh and Deacon, she asked, "Are we sure the bug is working?"

Kayleigh replied, "The answer to that remains the same as it was the other three times you inquired. Yes, it's been sending back the appropriate signal to confirm it's alive. We won't know more until we activate it for real, and we're not going to do that until the meeting time. Unless you want to risk having it discovered before then. Which would be dumb, even for you."

Diana scowled at the back of the blonde woman's head. "You're aware that, technically, I'm your boss, right? Maybe show some respect now and again?"

"Ha. Good one. I always said you were funny. Deacon doesn't agree."

Diana sighed inwardly. Sometimes, despite all the positive moments they'd had working together, the desire to slap Kayleigh in the back of the head was well-nigh overwhelming.

Cara laughed. "Respect is pretty hard to come by around here. It's weird how often intelligent, competent people turn out to be smart asses, as well."

Deacon replied, "Right? Seriously, she's intolerable."

Kayleigh retorted, "Don't insult the boss like that. Anyway, you're not one to talk. I mean, the stories I could tell."

Cara, Deacon, and Diana all simultaneously declared, "Don't." Kayleigh laughed, and Diana continued, "I read one minute until meeting time."

Agreement came from the others, and after forty-five seconds had passed, Kayleigh said, "Activating."

The room's speakers immediately gave them the sound of Richardson's office. A buzz signaled a call from his assistant, who announced through a tinny speakerphone, "Senator Borowski is here. Shall I show her in?"

His deep baritone replied, "Yeah, thanks." The gruffness was out of his voice when he spoke next. "Hello, Stella, take a seat. Want a drink?"

She replied, "Coffee would be great."

He said, "Make it two, thanks," clearly addressing his assistant. They heard the door close, then Richardson commented, "So, major events, eh?"

Diana sensed that the woman was probably frowning. "It's appalling how they've treated Finley. I mean, he's a *senator*. What's to stop Serrano from doing the same thing to us if he was willing to do it to him?"

A placating edge entered Richardson's tone. "Well, first

off, we're not consorting with terrorists. That's a significant differentiator right there. Second, I'm sure you've gathered some intel to keep our buddy Kevin in his place. I know I have."

Borowski replied, "I've got some. Not as much as I'd like, that's for certain."

Richardson said, "He's far cleaner on paper than you'd expect. His skeletons are well-buried. There's sure to be stuff there if we keep digging, though. Anyway, back to Finley. The hotel they're keeping him in is a decent one. As far as house arrest goes, it's a pretty nice gig, all things considered."

"Think they'll prosecute him?"

Richardson sighed, then delayed answering as the sounds of the assistant arriving with coffees took over the channel. When the door *clicked* closed again, he said, "I imagine Serrano will let everything go back to normal and keep a close eye on him. Having dirt on the senator is probably as useful for him as it is for us the other way around."

"Glad I'm not Aaron." A note of anger entered Borowski's voice. "I can't believe after all that effort, Serrano and his people *still* almost lost Bates."

Diana thought she was talking about capturing him until Richardson said, "Well, they couldn't have known he had some kind of drug capsule implanted."

Her eyes widened, and she turned to Cara. The other woman had a similar look of shock and alarm on her face. Richardson continued, "Thank heaven they were close enough to Walter Reed for Army medics to get over there in time."

Diana's heart fell back into a mostly normal rhythm at those words. Borowski asked, "Have you heard a prognosis?"

He replied, "Serrano's word is that if Bates regains consciousness, he'll probably be fine. The medics said there's no guarantee that will happen."

Borowski's voice was businesslike and emotionless now. "They give odds?"

"Sixty-forty, for. He's not stable enough to be moved yet, either."

The woman sighed. "Could be worse. But could be better, too. This was a colossal screwup."

Richardson replied, "I'll make sure Serrano is completely aware of that when the oversight committee meets. Speaking of which, we need to talk about strategy for that meeting. Our friend Kevin wants us to chip away at the authority of everyone who isn't us. Claims we're the only ones he can trust."

Borowski responded with a derisive chuckle. "He assumes we're stupid enough to believe that, too, which shows he's not as bright as he thinks he is."

"Exactly. So, let's figure out how to turn it to our advantage."

Diana rose without a word and stalked out of the cabin, her vision covered in a red haze of rage. If she were smart, she'd go to her quarters and grab Fury, relying on the sword to help her deal with the negative energy swirling inside her. While that would be functional, it wouldn't be satisfying. Instead, she went to the training room and dragged the heavy bag attached to the ceiling out on its track, giving her space to work.

She started with simple punches, then advanced into elbow strikes and back fists. With each pop of her body against the bag, she imagined it was Kevin Serrano she was fighting and took pleasure in imagining how each blow would've broken some part of his body. The punches weren't enough to dissipate her rage, though, and she mixed in kicks and knee smashes, shouting at each one's point of impact.

She coated her limbs with force to protect them as she continued to batter the heavy object, threading more magic into her muscles and bones to increase her speed and power. Diana lost herself in the imagined combat, continuing to abuse the bag until, with one giant scream, she channeled her strength and power into a double-fisted punch that sent the bag flying. Its chain snapped from the force of the blow. She winced, waiting for the inevitable crash as it broke something important, but only a soft rustle met her ears.

She opened her eyes to find Cara standing nearby, the heavy bag on the floor at her feet. "Feeling better, boss?"

Diana panted a little, trying to regain her breath. "A little, maybe. Still, if I get my hands on Serrano, I'm going to beat him to a pulp and bury the remains so deep they'll never be found."

Cara nodded. "I'm going to help you. To that end, Deacon has an idea to share."

Diana pushed sweaty hair out of her face and followed her second-in-command back to the techs' cabin. As soon as they entered, Deacon explained, "I can take a run at the security at Walter Reed hospital. They have enough systems running that I ought to find a way in, especially if they awarded any of it to the lowest bidder. Once in the system, I might find something useful."

Diana nodded. "Is it risky?"

"Very, since I'll be looking for specific information rather than creating a path to access the system later."

"Okay. Cara, pull up everyone in. Put the Castle on high alert. If they notice him, we want to be prepared for an attack. Make sure Khan's got essential systems rigged to blow."

Cara nodded. "Pack and portal?"

Diana replied, "Yeah, anything we can easily roll out of here into storage, do it, in case we have to leave in a hurry." She turned to the infomancer. "Do your thing, Deke. I'm counting on you. Get me something that will lead us to Bryant."

CHAPTER SEVENTEEN

Deacon popped the top on a soda can and quaffed the root beer in a series of loud gulps. His caffeine level was already sufficient, his nerves already wired from that plus the challenge that awaited him. Now he needed to be sure he wouldn't get too dehydrated during however long it took him to crack into the Walter Reed Medical Center's systems.

Diana had departed, fortunately. He'd feared she would stay and watch over his shoulder, and that was pressure he didn't need. Kayleigh had intervened and pushed her out, none too subtly. *Which is one of the many reasons I adore her.*

He focused on the computer system in front of him, establishing his magical link with it and losing himself in his custom interface as he made the transition from "meatspace" to the virtual world.

His viewpoint switched to an illusory technological landscape. It was a mix of solids and wireframes, somewhere between *Tron* and *Blade Runner*. He'd already figured out the location of the servers he wanted, but instead of heading directly there, he detoured, dragging his signal over nodes across several continents.

Deacon rerouted through as many as he could while still maintaining adequate response time to deal with whatever might come. He judged that the path would be sufficient to provide two or three seconds to react to a trace before it could make its way back to him. In the expanded timeframe of the virtual world, that would be more than enough to block and evade an enemy's effort to find his location.

This run was pretty much the opposite of how he preferred to do things. Normally, like when he'd broken into the D.C. traffic cameras, he liked to execute the hack and stay quiet for as long as possible. That allowed the infomancers who opposed him to believe they'd pushed him out of the system, which would inevitably lead to them letting down their guard. Thus, most of his primary runs inserted a dependable path into the server for later use.

Today, though, he needed to come back with information, specifically where the medics had gone when they'd responded to a call to assist Bryant. The boss wouldn't accept any delays, and to be fair, he wouldn't either. It would be riskier, as he'd told Diana, but the reward was worthy of the danger. *Even if it meant we had to leave the base, getting Bryant back would be worth it.*

He made his way into the webserver of one of the many companies that handled work outsourced by the hospital. It was a reality of the modern age that no business did all their internal coding, which he could use to his advantage. In this case, it was an insurance tracking software with a vulnerability, a bloated mess of code that Deacon easily sliced through to gain a foothold inside the Walter Reed systems.

Once there, he hit the obvious places where he might find something: ambulance dispatch, personnel records, and emergency room admissions. None of those provided a lead, which was more or less as he'd expected. *All right, then, time to get dirty.*

He found a connection that looked well-protected, appearing in his virtual vision as a heavy door marked "Medical Corps Only" with a camera above it, a keypad beside it, and a pair of soldiers standing guard. The lifelessness in the figures told him they represented a simple firewall, or at best, an AI that would respond to an effort to get in the door.

He ducked into a nearby room, which in the real world was him activating a concealment routine while he followed up with a disguise program. When he walked out of the chamber, he was a full bird colonel in the Army, with insignia and medals appropriate to the Medical Corps.

As he approached the door, the twin soldiers saluted but didn't otherwise acknowledge him. He pulled his ID tag from the lanyard around his neck and put it up against the code reader. The door slid open as his hacking software took care of that layer of defense, and he strode forward.

Once he got through the doorway, the simulation changed, signifying that heavier, more resistant code lay ahead. Had it been weaker, his hospital sim-slash-metaphor would've continued. Instead, the surrounding area had turned to stone, the floors underneath scuffed and faded linoleum, and the overhead lighting no longer institutional fluorescent but high function, low style work lights.

He recognized it immediately as a modified version of the dam installation Pierce Brosnan's James Bond had invaded to kick off *Goldeneye*. His uniform remained unaltered since apparently, the system was okay with 007 in disguise. He didn't imagine the simulation would bear any other similarity to that movie. The hospital's defenses had configured the interaction as a military base, and his magic and technology had rendered it into one he was familiar with.

He strode forward, looking like he belonged there, and pulled a pair of glasses from a pocket. They showed him an overlay of the standard detection modes when he put them on, searching for cameras, traps, and other security devices. After almost a full minute of walking without any notable change in scene, he realized the defenses had duped him into a loop. *Okay, so someone on the other side is at least decent at what they do.*

A loop was a common defensive trap, one that was applied automatically against an invader. It provided an illusion of progress while the victim was locked in a holding space, awaiting a response from higher-level security. The time differential meant he'd only been in that situation for a second or so in the outer world so he wasn't overly worried.

Likely, the system wouldn't signal an enemy infomancer that quickly because it would deal with low-level intrusion attempts on a more or less constant basis. It would try its programmed solutions before calling for help.

He stopped and pulled a pack of chewing gum from his pocket. He took out the five sticks and pressed them in a line against the wall, where they adhered instantly. Then he stepped away to a safe distance and pushed the winding stud on his classic analog watch three times. The explosive detonated, blasting a hole in the wall barely large enough for him to slide through. He grinned. "Gadgets. I *love* gadgets."

His various software tools always took on interesting forms in the shared simulations he wound up in, which was part of his job's fun. Even at moments like this, when so much depended on his success—literally life or death— he never failed to enjoy the work. Slipping through the opening let him into an entirely different sort of space, from a corridor to a large, wide-open hangar filled with military vehicles, crates of weapons and ammunition, and dozens of soldiers walking around.

He'd arrived in an inventory system by the look of his surroundings. Given the skills of the military's logistics people, it was one of the more dangerous spots he could've landed in. The defenses here would be far more attuned to intrusion than in less essential systems and much quicker to call for assistance. It was possible, maybe even likely, that an infomancer was somewhere inside the area with him, doing their everyday job, which meant he needed to be very careful to avoid being spotted by them.

Deacon ducked into a corner and altered his disguise, pulling off his medals and slapping new rank patches on the uniform to make him resemble another security guard. He strode along the perimeter, looking this way and that, doing his level best to appear identical to the others patrolling the area.

The glass window two stories above caught his eye, but he was careful not to stare at it. More likely than not, he'd find what he needed there since it was the standard movie location for a central control room. *My magic at work.*

He spotted an exit on the chamber's far side, in a logical position to hold a stairwell or elevator that would take him to that upper-level windowed room. He continued on his path and avoided changing his actions other than an occasional extra look at that opening.

He finally reached it and strode through, discovering a concrete staircase leading upward in a series of switchbacks. Unfortunately, it also held a pair of guards. They lifted their AK-47s and demanded to see his identification, plus an explanation for why he'd entered a restricted zone.

Okay. Here we go.

CHAPTER EIGHTEEN

Deacon reached back and slapped a button that hadn't been there a moment before, summoning a door to seal off the stairwell from the larger room. It was appropriate enough to the simulation that hopefully none of the AIs outside would notice his alteration.

Instead of reaching for his ID, he quick-drew the silenced pistol from his holster and delivered a controlled pair to each guard, one bullet in the chest and another in the head, dropping them. That action wouldn't have been possible if they'd been infomancers, but artificial intelligences couldn't move as fast as he could in a simulation he partially controlled.

He dragged the men under the stairwell, shoved them into the shadows, and grabbed one of their rifles. He holstered his pistol and headed up the stairs. It only took him ten seconds to realize that it had routed him into another loop, an endless staircase. He didn't have any more explosives with him, but he did have James Bond's patented laser watch. He pressed and held the button to carve a seam in one of the walls, then stepped through it to another set of stairs. This one had landings and doors above.

The first landing marked the second floor and had a door with a small window set in it, protected by a metal grate on both sides. He peered through from one edge, careful not to be noticed. It led onto a floor that looked very much like a hospital. *Probably the main server for the Army Medical Corps.*

The information *might* be in there, but the presence of the obvious control room still drew him upward. In the arcane interaction between his magic and the computer system, the object he sought was usually in some recognizable destination. *Like at the top of the damn Donkey Kong climb.* If he didn't find it in the control room, this would be the next place he'd look.

Now that he'd taken direct action by eliminating some of the system's defenses, he increased his efforts to find defensive devices and cameras. It was extremely likely his attack on the pair of guards had ratcheted up the security level. That meant his disguise would be increasingly vulnerable as the systems devoted more power and attention to piercing it.

He passed three along the way and disabled them by cutting the cables attaching them to the wall. It would create a trail, but he had no other good options to deal with them given the scenario's limitations. *Unfortunately, no magical veils exist in James Bond's universe.*

He reached the next floor, where a single guard stood outside a heavy, featureless door. The man demanded, "Identification, soldier." It was obvious from his body movements that this was a live person's avatar, probably a lower level infomancer handling security on the system.

A worker bee, rather than one of the elites. His enlisted insignia supports that. Simulations frequently drew inspiration from the real world that turned out to be useful in understanding those systems.

He couldn't risk the sound of even a muffled gunshot. Instead, he slipped in and drove his fist into the other man's throat. His opponent shifted aside enough to take it in the neck, saving his life. The blow still rendered him unable to speak for a moment, which was its purpose.

Deacon stepped forward and grabbed the man's shoulders, yanking him down so the knee he thrust into the guard's solar plexus was all the more effective. He finished by slamming the unfortunate man's head against the stone wall behind him. His foe slumped, and Deacon quietly lowered him to the floor.

He turned his attention to the door. It had a number pad beside it rather than a simple ID recognition sensor. He withdrew a keychain from his pocket and pointed the small, attached capsule at the keypad.

The cylinder had a tiny protrusion on the top, and when he pressed it, minute specks of shining glitter spewed out of it. The coating showed button usage by sticking better to the oil deposited on the ones most frequently used.

Deacon entered that information into his code breaker, which then worked in silence for several seconds. First, it calculated its guess at the most likely codes, then put together an algorithm to go through all the possibilities as quickly as possible if its presumption proved incorrect.

Since he was entering the potentially most secure area in the simulation, it was almost certain that too many mistaken entries would increase the security level again. Taking too long to input the right one after beginning the process would too.

Reinforcements charging in from above and below to join me in the control room would not be an improvement. If the device didn't work, it would force him to resort to brute force, smash open the pad and try to wire it himself, figuratively speaking. That would likely draw an even bigger defensive response. Brute force wasn't a thing that often worked in computer hacking, despite what a legion of films and television representations suggested.

He hit the button to activate the breaker, and the LEDs on the black box flickered as it attempted to hack the number pad. The door popped open, but not before he heard footsteps coming from both directions on the stairs. He grabbed a grenade from the fallen soldier's belt, pulled the pin, and stepped through the doorway.

Deacon tossed the canister into the stairwell, then yanked the door closed behind him. It went off on the other side, hopefully demolishing the keypad and probably at least causing the reinforcements to take cover. He turned to face the room. A dozen technicians sitting at various tasks and one officer in a dress uniform, right down to the medallioned service cap, filled it.

Deacon hosed the office with the AK, firing until the magazine ran dry. One tech remained miraculously unhit, but a shot from Deacon's silenced pistol took care of him. Behind the infomancer, shouts demanding entrance accompanied pounding on the door.

He smiled at the officer and pointed toward the corner of the room. "I'm here for that." The *Goldeneye* device lay nestled in a black case that sat on top of a control panel.

The other man cracked his knuckles and waved. His dress uniform transformed into tactical pants and a t-shirt, with heavy boots instead of polished shoes. Not to be outdone, Deacon copied the gesture and wardrobe selection. Rather than a plain black top, his was a concert shirt from The Clash. *Seems appropriate for the moment.*

His foe said, "Impressive work getting this far. I'll have to review our procedures and figure out what weaknesses you exploited so someone better can't make use of them later. Of course, there's no way you're going to escape, even if you defeat me."

Deacon felt the pressure in his mind that signaled the start of a trace program seeking him, doubtless triggered by the other man's words. He shrugged. "No way you'll get what you're looking before I wipe you out, take your fancy toy, and blow out of here."

The other man held his hands wide and taunted, "Bring it on."

Deacon whipped his pistol up and fired a triple burst at the man's face, but his target was already in motion. His opponent's pistol cleared its holster with impressive speed and forced Deacon to move to the side, circling as they traded shots. The situation held until his gun *clicked* empty. He threw it at the other man and followed it, bracing himself for the impact of bullets.

No such sensation came. His throw had been good enough to make the man flinch, and now he was too close for the pistol to come back into range. He reached out with his left hand to grab the gun barrel, then punched his enemy's wrist with his right. The blow numbed his foe's hand and weakened his grip. Deacon threw the weapon aside.

He shifted his leg to absorb the knee strike his enemy had aimed at his groin on his thigh, then jabbed him with an elbow in the torso, clearing a little space between them. He snapped out a kick, but his opponent stepped sideways to avoid it and punched Deacon's leg, catching him in the knee. The limb failed when he set it down, and he turned the collapse into a roll toward the case.

The other man snarled, "Get away from there," and ran forward. He grabbed Deacon by the shirt and hurled him across the room to slam into the wall. He curled up in a ball to protect himself from the impact and surged back to his feet the moment he hit the floor, noting that the world's physics were more movie than reality.

That explained why the thrown gun had worked and why he'd been tossed so effortlessly through the air. It was also a wrinkle that suited him perfectly.

Deacon made a long leap, crossed more space than he would've been able to in the real world, and snapped out a sidekick at the other man. His foe pulled his arms in to block, but that wasn't enough to stop him from being knocked back against the console in front of the window. Deacon landed cleanly and spun into a back hook kick, but the man ducked underneath it and tried another punch at his knee. Deacon shifted the blow's angle and brought an ax kick down at his enemy's neck, forcing his opponent to abandon his counterattack and roll away.

His foe's evasion gave Deacon a clear path to the case.

He ran to it, snapped it closed, and grabbed it by the handle. He turned back to find that his enemy had produced a rifle from somewhere and was aiming it solidly at Deacon's chest while backing toward the door, which he would surely unlock to let the rest of the defenders in.

He saw only one solution, as unfortunate as it seemed. His torso twisted as he hurled the case at the large window, which shattered easily, consistent with the system's altered reality. Then he jumped up on the console and dove out after it.

His control over the simulation was sufficient to ensure a large vehicle would be waiting below, so he only fell about ten feet before slamming onto the top of a tall truck. He rolled down to the top of its cab, then its hood, and finally landed on the hangar floor two feet away from the case. *I love it when movie rules are in effect.*

The surrounding area was chaos, with guards shouting and fire coming from above. He ran toward one of the cars, an open-top Jeep, and feinted as though he would jump inside. Gunfire converged on it, and he bolted in the other direction as the barrage caused the vehicle to explode. That detonation set off several others all around the area, and Deacon used the destruction's distraction to make a run for it.

One guard stepped into his path and raised a weapon, but Deacon leapt into the air with a shout and came down on the blocker in a flying smash. One fist landed on the man's face, the other on his neck, and both of his knees slammed into the unfortunate soldier's chest. He fell back on the floor. Deacon landed on top of him, smashing the fragile bones of the guard's ribcage.

The fallen man spat out a mouthful of blood, and Deacon offered a mental nod of appreciation to whoever had coded the simulation so extensively. *Now, maybe work on buffing up the defenses instead of going for dramatic effect.*

He'd been keeping a timer on the trace in the back of his mind. It was probably about halfway to him. Rather than running from the simulation as his avatar, which would permit him to leave a hidden door active, he sent a signal to his body in meatspace, and its foot kicked out to activate the instant disconnect button.

The infomancer slumped in his chair, as exhausted as if he'd been in the fight and dying of thirst. He reached down to the cooler, pulled out a Coke and drained it, then popped the top on a Dr. Pepper to sip from it more calmly.

When his heart had calmed, and his mental focus had returned, he hit the buttons to start decrypting the information he'd extracted from the server. If his skills were up to the task, as they usually were, somewhere within that data would be an important record. One that would lead them to the medics, or to the location they'd been dispatched to, or to some other piece of the puzzle that would at least give them a starting place to find Bryant.

CHAPTER NINETEEN

Diana had returned to the techs' cabin clad in full combat gear, including Fury in its back sheath. Now and again, she reached over her shoulder to touch the hilt, drawing confidence and calm from her connection to the sentient being inside. Deacon was on her left, hard at work optimizing his signal strength and communication to their planned area of operation, the one he'd found with his hack into the Walter Reed computers.

To her right, Kayleigh was manipulating a pair of drones. The video feeds were visible on the large monitor above her station.

The first was up very high, offering a top-down view of the industrial park the Army medics had visited to treat Bryant. The area was similar to where they'd traced the vehicles from the kidnapping but was in a different part of the city. *Serrano's smart, keeping his resources spread out so no one can easily connect them. Probably has shell corporations and all that garbage, too.*

The other drone was flying about three stories above

roof height for the buildings in the area and maintaining a distance. Its powerful optic customization provided an exterior view of the warehouse that was the evening's target. Thermal imaging showed nothing from the interior.

Diana chose to believe that was a function of the technology's limitations over such a range rather than a sign that Bryant was no longer inside. She simply couldn't accept the notion that their only clue might turn out to be wrong or outdated.

As the drone circled, a wireframe overlay appeared on the image, marking cameras at several places on the building to maintain good coverage in all directions. A couple of them pointed up, a greater than average nod to keeping the space secure from drones as well.

Kayleigh said, "The only entries appear to be at ground level. A human-sized door on each end and four garage doors on each of the long sides. Pretty basic storage warehouse, at least from the outside. Three stories high…might have a second or third floor in there."

She looked back over her shoulder, and Diana noted the concern on her face. "You'll probably find more defenses and alarms inside, of course."

Diana nodded. "We'll deal with all that when we get there. Whatever they have, whatever it takes." She wanted to push her team into action immediately but knew that spending a bit longer watching the place before they did would give them valuable information.

She reluctantly pushed down her desire for motion yet again. The area around the warehouse was busy, unexpectedly so given the hour, with trailer trucks moving in and out on a steady basis.

Cara stepped into the room and reported, "The team's good to go." After a glance at the monitors, she continued, "Looks like a popular place."

Diana frowned. "It is, annoyingly so. Even with a veil, it won't be easy to sneak up on foot."

Her second-in-command chuckled. "I have a feeling you're about to make a decision that will put a smile on Hank's face."

She grinned at the other woman, finding at least one positive in the situation. "Deacon. We're going to need two trucks."

A half-hour later, Diana was in the passenger seat of an eighteen-wheeler and rigging the network enhancer to the dashboard while Hank drove. The rest of her team was inside the attached trailer, geared up and ready to assault the building.

This was the second truck they'd visited, spending only enough time at the first to attach the network enhancer so Deacon could drive it remotely, as well. The infomancer had promised he had plenty of programs for cracking vehicles, and all he needed was a way in. The enhancers made that possible.

She asked, "Deke, are you sure you can drive two of these things? They're rather bigger than drones. Plus, you'll have to shift manually."

"As easily as breathing."

Kayleigh interrupted, "Truck one is fifteen seconds from target location."

Deacon would park it at the far end of the building from where they planned to make their incursion. Ideally, the unexpected appearance would draw some eyeballs in that direction.

Hank took the truck through an extra quartet of turns to delay its arrival at the warehouse until the other was in place. Their rig wouldn't stop. The team would simply bail out and move while Deacon took over and drove the borrowed vehicle away.

Kayleigh provided a countdown, and Diana monitored the vehicles' positions on the overhead map in her display. Then she jumped out the side door at the appropriate moment, landed cleanly, and jogged away from the truck, which continued rolling. Her team gathered around her.

Diana cast a veil, then paused to see if a reaction was imminent. When nothing occurred, she said, "As planned. Do it."

Diana ran forward with Rath, Tony, and Cara, heading for a featureless expanse of wall while the rest of her team moved away on a diagonal. Her sensors still couldn't pick up any heat signals from within the building, which was starting to concern her, but this part of the plan wouldn't change even if no one awaited them inside.

When they arrived, Tony and Cara got to work pushing incendiary cord into place to outline an arched shape on the wall. Her glasses flipped through detection modes, confirming that the skin of the building was thin metal attached to a frame in much the same way that drywall went over studs. The location was for storage, not defense, which was a lucky break for her and her team.

She looked up. Hank, Anik, and Sloan were almost up

the side of the building, courtesy of small motors on their belts assisting their climb up a chain attached to a powerful magnet they'd launched to the building's roof with an air gun. When Tony and Cara finished outlining, Diana said, "Let's take a look."

Her second-in-command pulled a tool out of her belt, affixed a drill head to it, and made a small hole in the building's metal wall. Cara threaded the fiber-optic camera out of her sleeve and through the opening, and the image popped up on Diana's display. It showed a large empty space lit by work lights, with a chamber in the middle that looked like a modest one-story room with a flat roof.

Diana muttered, "Weird. But if they have him, that's probably where he'll be."

Hank reported, "Camera shows nothing below us. We're clear to move."

Diana replied, "Acknowledged. Glam, we good?"

The tech's response was confident. "Ready here."

"Deke?"

"Distraction is in place, and the other truck is idling nearby. I detect no internal systems for me to access. In fact, no signals at all coming from the building. If they have an alarm system, it's hard-wired."

Diana nodded. It wasn't perfect, but it was as good as they were likely to get. "Okay. We are 'Go' to breach in fifteen seconds from mark."

The countdown appeared in her glasses. Diana readied herself to move, sliding her left arm into a tall riot shield that Tony had carried for her and gripping her grenade launcher tightly in both hands. A wish for an extra arm flitted through her mind so she'd have a hand free to ensure Fury's steadying presence was with her through the battle to come. *That doesn't matter. Nothing matters, except getting in, grabbing Bryant, and getting out without losing anyone.*

When the timer hit zero, the incendiary cord burned a hole in the wall, and Diana ran through with her team a step behind her.

CHAPTER TWENTY

As Diana entered the warehouse, the sound of metal crashing came from one side as the team above cut through the roof and the detached portion dropped. She dashed to the far left of the space with Rath at her right, then Cara and Tony. Hank and Anik would fill out the front rank as they advanced through the building, with Sloan as their reserve.

She ordered, "Face, find a good spot to hide, and be ready to throw a force shield around whatever that room is if we meet any kind of response. We don't want a random act of violence to hurt the person we're here to save."

Sloan replied, "Affirmative."

Diana imagined he would fade toward the far side. She'd already spotted several locations he could use to hide where the shadows were deeper than others. *So that's taken care of.*

The warehouse itself was echoing and empty, apart from the structure in the middle. Kayleigh's guess that it might contain a second or third level proved true. A catwalk ran around the structure's perimeter halfway up with a small office on that level at the building's opposite end.

Cara said, "I'm getting a bad vibe here."

Diana replied, "Me, too."

Rath added, "Me, three." His voice lacked its normal playfulness, which was enough to cause her to pay attention to their shared concern.

She called, "Hold," and peered ahead carefully, letting her glasses run through their detection modes yet again. The structure in the center showed electricity flowing around the walls but emitted no heat signatures, no sounds, and nothing else that any of her scans could sense.

The riot shield had grown heavy on her left arm, a sign of tension, and Diana's hands clenched on the grenade launcher. *Nothing for it but to keep moving and see what we get.*

When the change came, it was sudden and drastic, a perfect tactical play. The soft sounds of grenade launchers going off offered a short prelude to canisters sailing out at them from the darkness ahead.

She shouted, "Scatter and defend," took her own advice, and ran toward the left side of the building. She let her launcher fall on its strap and waved to redirect any munitions coming her way with a blast of force magic. When the grenades went off, some were in the air, others were rolling on the floor, and unfortunately, some were near her team members.

Their glasses, goggles, and comms handled the flash-bang detonations, but not before a quick burst of light made her wince. The clouds emitted by the gas grenades were quickly blown away by her team's magic, sent flying upward back in the direction they'd come from.

A barrage of bullets followed the initial attack. Diana crouched behind her riot shield and looked for their enemies. The spell dropped, revealing three trios of uniformed figures and confirmed her momentary theory that the darkness might be magical in nature.

They fired bursts from assault rifles as they advanced, moving carefully forward while directing fire at her people, who used their shields to intercept the rounds. Rath was the only one of them without one, but he'd wisely sprinted over to hide with her. *Must not have been an illusion hiding them, or our bracelets would've alerted us. Shadow, maybe?*

"All right, our turn. Launch grenades." She gave the other side credit for their surprise attack and admitted to a deep frustration that they'd adopted the same heat signature masking technology her team's suits possessed.

She fired six canisters as fast as the drum would cycle them, aiming them in a high arc to land slightly behind the advancing figures. Unexpectedly, her munitions flew away to explode in a far corner of the building. A shimmering dome that protected them from Cara's and Tony's grenades covered the center team. Diana couldn't make out how the threesome on the far side defended themselves, but it appeared they, too, had successfully weathered the counterattack.

Cara snapped, "They have magicals on their side somewhere." Two more glowing barriers materialized, resulting in a magical shield covering all three teams, which their bullets passed through without any problem.

Diana shook her head, momentarily bereft of ideas for dealing with the changed situation. "We have to break through there, or we're going to lose our chance to rescue Bryant. We can't let them hide in their bubbles."

Hank replied, "Short of locking shields and advancing together, which probably wouldn't work anyway, trying to close with them will get us shot."

Cara added, "Concur. Boss?"

Diana heard the question encapsulated in that one word. "Yeah. We'll have to risk it. Pistols, shoot low, go for the legs."

Rescuing Bryant was important enough to her that she'd take any risk. While she would've preferred to take it on herself only and let her people remain clear of it, the scale of the battle made that impossible. She drew her pistol and started firing, aiming at the legs of those nearest. As soon as she did, though, the figures ahead of her reacted entirely unexpectedly.

One of them flew into the air, rocketing upward on what had to be a blast of force magic. The second reached toward a zone of shadow on the far right, and a large piece of metal flew out of it to interpose itself between that person and her potential bullets. The third simply vanished, going from visible to invisible in the space of a breath.

Tony said the words before she could. "Holy hell. They're *all* magicals."

Bullets flew. Diana ignored her advice and aimed at the one who was flying, making a low shot an additional challenge. The rest of her team would hopefully select targets that gave them a better opportunity to hit the mark. Rath was hurling grenades in a clatter, which detonated into smoke and glittering confetti.

She called, "Good idea, buddy. Everyone, we're not going to win a ranged battle. Pop smoke and get close." She holstered her pistol and grabbed canisters from her belt, tossing them forward one after the next. As they exploded, she pulled Fury from over her shoulder, threaded some magical strength into her left arm to help with the weight of the riot shield, and barreled into the smoke.

A yelp of pain came from her right, followed by Tony's moaned, "I'm hit." A low gasp sounded from him, and a fraught silence descended.

Cara swore vividly, but Diana couldn't see what was going on. The comms were filled with sounds of exertion, growls of anger, and more than one grunt and groan from the impact of a bullet into armor or flesh. Her right arm burned from where a round had carved a chunk out of it in passing. She stepped forward and found herself one-on-one with the enemy that had levitated the piece of metal in front of them.

Diana bared her teeth in a nasty grin, ready to start evening the odds. As she charged, Kayleigh's voice burst over the comm, suffused with alarm and surprise. "Sensors have picked up people on the island's surface. At least a dozen. I don't think they're tourists."

CHAPTER TWENTY-ONE

Anik fired several bullets to no effect and decided that his particular skills offered other possibilities that might better benefit the team. He faded backward, away from the front line, shifting toward a pool of darkness near the side. Hank shot at the enemy Anik had tangled with, distracting him, and no one else saw him relocate, as far as he could tell. He knelt and pulled open the top flap of the demolition pouch attached to his right leg, one of two he habitually carried.

The container produced detonators and explosives separated into smaller plastic containers. He jammed the latter into the former to create several remote-activated bombs. Anik peeled the adhesive off the back and stuck one to the wall, then dashed to the next area of darkness and did the same with another.

As he ran to a third, he announced, "Placing traps in the dark spots. If things get bad, manipulate your enemies into them. I'll be watching."

He ducked suddenly as an enemy soldier raced past

his position, thanking fate for the generalized darkness. The warehouse had sufficient illumination that their opponents weren't using low light tech, which was probably the only reason he was still alive. *Careful, chucklehead.*

His advance to the next was slower as he kept a careful eye open for enemies. Movement caught his attention, and he warned, "Watch out. Looks like at least one was hiding in the back. He's moving toward the front now."

Diana fed magic into her body to increase her speed and power, then slammed her riot shield with all her momentum behind it into the metal plate her opponent was using as a defense. It knocked the figure backward, and the improvised blocker clattered to the floor. Diana interposed Fury in the way of the lightning blast her opponent discharged at her, The sword sucking the spell in harmlessly. She ran forward, transitioning smoothly into a jumping side kick.

Her foe summoned force magic to knock Diana out of line, but the hurried reaction wasn't powerful enough to send her too far off course. Her feet hit the floor two feet away from her target, and she kicked back hard. Her heel connected with flesh and a female voice cried out in pain. *Equal opportunity scumbags. Awesome.*

She looked over her shoulder, leapt backward, and slammed an elbow into her opponent's chest. The woman recoiled, and Diana spun to hook her foe's legs out from underneath her. She landed on her back, and Diana punched her in the face. The shock glove's *snap* took the other woman out of the fight.

A quick burst of force pushed her back up to her feet, where a fireball was inches from her chest. Her anti-magic deflector absorbed the arcane fire with a loud *crack*. The dissipating flames revealed a surprised expression on the man who'd thrown it.

She lunged forward, trying to smash him in the head with the force-covered Fury, but he backpedaled and circled away to blast more fire at her. Diana tossed her shield to the side and counterattacked with a burst of ice at his boots.

He slipped, and while he focused on catching his balance, she closed and punched him in the neck. The stun discharge took him out of the fight at least momentarily. He moaned from his fallen position, not fully unconscious, but she had no time to finish him.

Instead, she launched herself in a shallow arc across the width of the warehouse to land next to a man who'd been moving with deliberate stealth toward where she'd last seen Sloan.

He reacted quickly to her arrival and swung his rifle butt around in a smash at her head. She leaned back to avoid it, and he kicked her stomach. Her body armor absorbed the blow.

His advance put her unexpectedly on the defensive as he led with a punch from his left fist. His right hand went for the gun in a thigh holster on that side. She smacked that wrist with Fury, breaking it, and took advantage of his momentary distraction to front-kick his stomach and create some distance between them.

She summoned electricity and blasted him, but he wrapped himself in a cocoon of force as he stumbled, fell, and rolled away from her. A bout of swearing from Cara made her jerk her head around. Her second-in-command had two enemies attacking her, one on either side.

Diana snapped, "Face, drop the shield and get Stark to someplace safe. Rambo, Croft, get in and get the package. Hercules, peel those two off Croft, and let's keep these assholes busy."

At Diana's command, Rath dashed for the structure in the center of the building. The enemy troops had been waiting for someone to do that because they disengaged and fell back, creating a human—*well, magical*—barrier. Rath ducked his head and ran forward, readying himself for their inevitable attack.

When it came in a barrage of fire and shadow, he shrank in a couple of steps. His gear dropped off as he shifted from three feet tall to a third of that. The edge of the magical wave caught him, but his deflector consumed it before it fell away. The change happened too quickly and was too unexpected for his opponents to react in any more useful way, and he was through the legs of one before they knew what was happening.

He laughed—a high-pitched sound at his small height—and grew, shifting from his tiny size to almost eight feet tall. He punched the door with both hands, then used the holes he'd made to rip it from its hinges and throw it at the people who'd tried to stop him. They were finally turning to see what had happened.

Within, Bryant lay on a medical table, attached to machines with tubes coming out of his arms. Rath growled and ducked inside, stepping into a protective position in front of the unconscious man.

***

Hank spotted Cara's predicament immediately and let out a growl that was equal parts pleasure and anger. He'd exchanged blows with one enemy, building up his magic pool. Baring his teeth in a grin as he ran, he reached up and slapped the front of his right shoulder, breaking the capsule contained there.

Magical energy flowed into his bloodstream, doubling his reserve and setting his senses afire. He smashed into Cara's nearest attacker, who saw him coming but didn't react soon enough to mount an effective defense.

The man had managed to put his rifle in the way, but that didn't bother Hank in the least. He punched his foe's stomach with his right hand, the magically powered blow lifting his opponent from his feet and sending him flying to crash into the warehouse's far wall. Cara threw up a wall of force to separate herself from the other attacker and bolted, headed off to obey Diana's orders, no doubt.

That left Hank eye-to-eye with a man holding a pistol in his right hand and a wand in his other. Bullets flew, but Hank ran in a serpentine toward his enemy, ducking and dodging. A pair caught him, one in the arm that stung more than a little and the other striking his vest and causing minimal discomfort.

The wand delivered a force blast that knocked him off his stride. He stumbled momentarily, then dove to the side as the man tried to shoot him again. The pistol *clicked* empty, and Hank grinned.

This time, the wizard summoned a wall of force to keep him away as he tried to close. He lifted his grenade launcher from where it hung on his chest and fired grenades in a high arc, trusting that the wall wouldn't reach the ceiling and thus would fail to protect the man's head.

Unfortunately, his foe proved adequate to the challenge, and the canisters bounced back at him. *Combat experience probably taught him that. Good for him, less good for me.*

He dashed to the left, selected a different opponent moving toward the central structure, and punched the man in the ribs. That blow used no magic but still stopped him in his tracks. Hank kicked the legs out from under the other man, upending him to slam hard on the floor. He stomped on his foe's shin, smashing it and ensuring he'd stay down. Then, burning with magical energy, he set his sights on the next upright enemy and ran to engage him.

A chill flowed through him as Kayleigh reported, "They've found the tunnel. This isn't good, people."

CHAPTER TWENTY-TWO

S loan had remained in the rear while the others reacted to Diana's orders, circling to find a relatively enemy-free path to reach their fallen teammate. Tony was on the floor, not moving, with blood puddling next to him. The nearest opponents were on the side Anik had run to. He said, "Khan, give me a distraction."

A second later, a pair of explosions went off on that side, one after the other. Sloan didn't think they were close enough to any enemies to hurt them, but that wasn't the point. He rushed forward and grabbed Tony, lifting him in a fireman's carry that made his whole body ache. *Thank heaven it wasn't Hank who went down. I need to hit the weights.*

He cast a portal and ran through it, ending up in the bedroom of his busted lobbyist persona's apartment. The rift closed behind him, and he lowered Tony onto the bed. A quick check showed that he wasn't in imminent danger, or at least not so much that a couple of minutes would make a difference.

He had every confidence that enemies would be on the

way, that they'd left some sort of surveillance in place. He wouldn't be there long enough for it to matter. He ran into the closet, kicked through a false panel at the bottom, and pulled out an emergency pack. It held a pistol that he stuck in his waistband, some money and ID that he shoved in a pocket rather than leave behind, and a medkit.

He pulled the military clothing off Tony and wrapped bandages around his wounds in the process. None of them appeared to be life-threatening on their own. *Hooray for body armor.* Then he slid shorts and a t-shirt onto the unconscious man and changed his clothes to some that wouldn't inspire an immediate call to the police.

Finally, he lifted Tony again and portaled him to a hospital in Pittsburgh, having no better option given the severity of his wounds. He delivered him to the ER and proceeded to falsify the paperwork, hoping they'd see Tony as an innocent shooting victim rather than one of the government's most wanted terrorists. When he'd done as much lying on the forms as he could, he handed them in, walked outside for an alleged smoke, and portaled away.

After Sloan vanished from the warehouse with Tony over his shoulder, Diana wound up in the center of three enemies. She had no idea where two of them had come from. Perhaps they'd been behind veils, or maybe she'd lost her situational awareness while watching Rath smash into the room where Bryant *had* to be.

The troll was off-comm, which she hated right now, but

his gear wouldn't go that small. She whipped Fury in a wide arc, forcing one of her foes to retreat. The other two drew pistols, while the backpedaling one leveled his rifle at her.

Diana didn't see a way to defeat them, for they surely had anti-magic ammunition and were close enough to target her uncovered spots. She blasted herself upward on a rocket of force magic, but shadow and force struck her in midair.

Previous attacks had long since consumed her deflector, and despite the shield along her skin, the blast's power smashed her sideways to slam into the warehouse's metal wall. Her cocoon protected her somewhat from the impact, and she managed to soften her harsh landing on the floor with a quick burst of force, but the blow injured her leg, and she felt decidedly woozy.

A cold realization settled over her that she'd reached the moment she'd warned the others about. If she continued trying to protect the lives of the three people coming after her, she would most likely lose hers.

In another circumstance, she might've considered letting those chips fall where they may, although she wasn't one to quit, ever. With Bryant's life at stake and the rest of her team in danger, only one choice was possible. She'd lost Fury at some point in the preceding seconds, so her hands were free. She slapped the capsules on each of her shoulders, and her back arched as energy and healing poured into her.

Using magically enhanced speed, she drew her pistol from its holster, lifted it, and squeezed off a triple burst into each of the enemies closing on her, aiming center mass. Her bullets all struck, and the trio fell backward one after the next.

She shifted her internal magic from speed to strength as she got back to her feet. A stumble took her toward Fury, and she ejected the pistol's magazine as she moved, automatically replacing it with another and readying the gun for more action.

Cara bolted for the room in the middle, blasting an enemy who tried to block her with a jolt of lightning that wrapped around the force shield he'd only put in front of him. *Amateur.* It distracted him enough that the protection died. She smashed an elbow into his alarmed face as she went by, possibly harder than strictly necessary. *That'll help you remember the lesson, scumbag.*

He fell backward, rebounded off the structure, and presumably hit the floor. She was already inside and didn't see his fate. She took in the scene in an instant, considering whether she'd be better transporting him on the stretcher or having Rath carry him through the portal back to the castle where medical gear awaited.

At that moment, Kayleigh's voice came over the comm with the confirmation she'd feared. "They've brought multiple assault teams. We have no chance of holding them off and are abandoning the base. The Castle has fallen."

Cara summoned a portal to the receiving room in Ruby's bunker, their backup plan for Bryant's medical needs, and pushed the stretcher through. She grimaced at the realization that she'd have to stay with Bryant and leave the others to the battle, but she didn't know if anyone else would be in the bunker, so she'd need to take care of him. She called, "Croft and the package are out," and sealed the portal behind her.

Rath had been watching the door as Cara took care of Bryant. When a figure appeared before she'd gotten him out of there, he charged ahead to take it on. A searing line of magic slammed him in the shoulder, the continuous bolt of fire trying to burn through his skin. *Fortunately, troll hide is tough. Although it's true, we don't like fire much.*

He abandoned subtlety, grabbed the man in a bear hug, and continued his forward rush. His arms flexed, squeezing the breath out of his captive and holding him close so he couldn't defend himself.

Another enemy appeared along his path. Rath laughed as he hurled the man he was holding forward like he'd seen basketball players do, a chest pass that slammed the one into the other and sent both of them falling damaged to the floor.

He spun to take stock of the situation. Roughly two-thirds of their enemies were down, but the remaining ones were moving in the same direction, clearly planning to regroup. He charged toward Diana's position, figuring that was the smartest and safest place he could be.

Diana closed her hand around Fury's hilt and lifted the sword, no longer bothering to coat it with force. She was ready to skewer anyone who tried to stop her from getting her team out of there.

Deacon announced, "Incoming, north, friendly."

She turned her head in that direction as one of the tractor-trailers slammed through the wall with a screeching howl of metal, sending the enemies nearby scattering. Even the ones on the floor—those still conscious, anyway—crawled to get away from the sudden threat.

Diana shouted, "Everybody out of the pool, stat," opened a portal, and motioned Rath through it. She followed him, and it closed a moment later, leaving them momentarily alone at their former safe house on Cape Cod. She didn't wait long enough to catch her breath, unsure of whether the house might be under surveillance.

A gesture created another portal, revealing Ruby's bunker on the opposite side. She ran through, then burst from the room as confirmation that the rest of her team was safe in their escape spots came through the comm.

Her steps slowed as she walked over to where Cara looked down at Bryant. She put her hand on his shoulder, almost unable to believe he was there without the sense of physical contact. She watched his chest, which rose and lowered rhythmically.

He's here. He's here. We did it. Rath's hand found hers, and she squeezed it. Her closest family was whole again.

CHAPTER TWENTY-THREE

A few moments after Diana's arrival, Ruby showed up with Nylotte and another woman. The *Mirra* of the Mist Elves explained, "I got the alert from Kayleigh automatically when the intruders threatened the base. Guess I'm still in your systems." She tapped the ear where she wore one of their comms. "Sounded like big trouble. I figured you might need some serious help, so I popped over to Oriceran and called for Nylotte."

Diana's teacher added, "This is Kyrstar. She has a talent for healing." The woman in question was also a Drow, probably younger than Nylotte, although that woman's agelessness left any such conclusion in doubt. The pair moved straight to Bryant's stretcher, which occupied the center of the room.

Kyrstar clucked her tongue. "We need to move him into a quieter space before I can help him."

Ruby offered, "Let's use my workshop," and led the way in there, using magic to push the heavy table to one side so the wheeled stretcher could fit inside.

Diana avoided looking down at Bryant again. She'd already seen as much of his unconsciousness as she could handle. After the initial glow of reunion, each new glance at his too-still form sent anxiety shooting through her. Her hand found its way to Fury's hilt as often as reasonably possible, and the sentient sword helped her to keep a lid on her spiraling emotions.

The chamber only had enough space to fit Nylotte, the healer, Ruby, Diana, and Bryant's stretcher. Kyrstar pulled a stool up to his feet and closed her eyes. The flow of magic from her toward her patient filled the room almost to the point of claustrophobia. She stayed that way for a handful of minutes while the rest of them remained silent, exchanging occasional glances of concern or reassurance.

Finally, Kyrstar's eyes opened, and she blew out a breath as if she'd exerted herself. "The good news is I sense him in there, not far from the surface. The drug interaction has put parts of his mind out of reach, but I believe we can fix those connections and thus fix him."

She reached into the backpack she'd worn into the room and pulled out a bag, which she unfolded to reveal a dozen small metal canisters. Each was in a loop to keep them in place. She chose one, withdrew a leaf, and extended it to Nylotte. "Under his tongue, please."

Nylotte accepted it and did as the other woman asked, which Diana thought might've been the first time she'd seen the always-superior Drow take instruction so pleasantly. The fact that such an amusing concept broke through her emotional walls jarred her into the sudden realization that she believed Bryant would be okay, now that Nylotte and her companion were on the case. *Friend? Partner? Lover? I wonder.*

All that flew out of her head as the healer put her palm on Bryant's bare ankle and muttered an incantation. His body spasmed and his eyes shot open in alarm. Nylotte held him down with one strong hand, and Diana leaned over to get into his line of sight. "It's okay. We've got you."

He smiled. "Never doubted." It came out slurred due to the leaf in his mouth, and his eyelids fluttered closed again.

She looked down at the healer, concerned, but the woman was calmly packing up her bag. Kyrstar advised, "Even with healing potions, he's going to be weak for a while. Whatever you all did to him, it wasn't kind. He should eventually make a full recovery."

Ruby asked, "So, are you a doctor, then?"

Nylotte gave a small snort. "Say instead that she's a warrior of a sort, with a penchant for healing others." She continued in a lower tone, "And getting herself into trouble."

Kyrstar snapped, "Sure, whine all you want. You know you'd be a mess without me."

Diana watched the interplay, her mouth trying to twitch into a smile that she suppressed for fear of annoying her mentor. Instead, she requested, "Nylotte, could I have a word with you in private?" The Drow nodded, and she escorted her into the storeroom that had been the techs' workspace. She closed the door. "What's the deal with your friend?"

Nylotte shook her head. "That would take far too long to tell. She's helping me with some things, and I'm helping her with some things. It works out. But I sense that's not what you want to talk to me about."

Diana leaned against the wall and let her head fall gently back to the hard surface, as well. "I feel like I've reached a point of no return. At the warehouse, when my people and I were in danger, I shot to kill, three rounds each at three people. I don't know if they're dead, but I *do* know we can't keep going on like this."

She tilted her head to meet the other woman's eyes. "Protecting our enemies to avoid being branded as criminals seems less than attractive, given that we've been branded as criminals anyway. Still, it feels like that's a big step and a considerable risk."

Nylotte nodded. "I understand. It's part of who you are to want to be loyal, even though those you offer your loyalty to feel no reciprocal commitment."

"True. It doesn't seem like something they should die for, though. Or, more specifically, that the people they manipulate into taking us on should die for."

The Drow shrugged. "I disagree, but I've always been quite satisfied to let people face the consequences of their choices. You could certainly come to Oriceran, as could your team. In fact, since I brought a healer, you owe me now. You'll have to pay me back with some time there to make it good."

Always an angle with you, lady. "Training?"

Nylotte shook her head. "Hunting."

Her serious tone gave Diana pause. "Hunting what?"

She didn't know if the other woman would've responded or what that response could've been because a knock on the door was followed immediately by Deacon opening it.

He reported, "I did my best to delay it, but the local police have received notification about Tony. They only have him listed as an ordinary shooting victim, though."

Diana pushed herself off the wall. "Nothing ordinary about Stark. We should get him moved before they come to interview him. Do you know if he's stable enough to travel?"

He followed her out into the main room. "He's still in ICU, so I don't think we can bring him here or anything. Unless the same healing that worked on Bryant would work on him."

Nylotte replied, "Doubtful. Kyrstar is a magical healer. It's woven into everything she does."

Ruby was sitting next to Idryll on the couch, absently petting the shapeshifter's hair. "I think I can help with that. There's a private clinic in Magic City that high rollers use when they want certain medical maladies to stay off the books. My family has a stake in the business, so there's no question about them keeping our secrets."

Kayleigh spoke up from across the room. "What kind of maladies?"

The Mist Elf shrugged. "Everything from chronic illnesses to overindulging in recreational pharmaceuticals. Gamblers sometimes have addictive personalities."

Diana nodded. "No judgment here. We're glad for the help. Sloan, Hank, go get Tony and take him to Ruby's place."

She gave the others tasks to do, as much to keep them busy as to accomplish things that needed doing, then made her way into the workshop. Only the healer remained, talking lightly with her patient. Diana asked, "So he's going to be okay?"

Kyrstar rose and slid past her toward the door, bumping into her as she maneuvered in the narrow room. "He should be fine. Intravenous fluids are a good idea. Keep them running. We want to flush all those chemicals out of his system.

"Someone should always be with him, just in case. At this point, rest and healing potions are what he needs." She smiled. "Plus, perhaps a friendly face."

The Dark Elf exited the room, and Diana pulled the stool the healer had been using forward so she was near Bryant's head. "Hi again, Bry-Bry."

He chuckled. "Ow. Everything hurts."

"Well, you did almost kill yourself. Idiot."

A sigh escaped him. "You would've done the same damn thing, and you know it."

She rested her hand on his arm and nodded. "You're right. I'm sure your choice protected us. How much do you know about what went down?"

"Virtually nothing."

"It's not too good." Diana explained that they'd lost the base, that Stark was injured, and that she might've killed one or more of the enemy in the warehouse. She finished up by summarizing, "I think the chances of us becoming part of the government again, ever, are minimal at best and falling by the second."

He'd taken the news well but was appropriately serious, given what they now faced. "Optimistic."

"Nylotte offered us a place on Oriceran. We could all go there, hike, camp, live off the land."

"Do you want to do that?"

She leaned against the stretcher, resting her head in her hand. "Part of me does. I think it's the same part that loves romance movies and other unrealistic fantasies."

He grinned. "There's the Diana I know. I was worried she was lost."

She straightened and gave a slow nod. "We have things to do here. The artifacts. The cult, whatever the hell is up with that. *Helping* people. Seriously, Rath would never let me get away with abandoning all that responsibility. I'd hear Spider-Man quotes all day and night, forever."

Bryant laughed, then cringed. "Laughing hurts. No jokes. Can't handle them yet."

"No promises. Do you agree?"

"I do. Looks like we're about to become vigilantes."

She gave a soft snort. "That sounds so much better than terrorists on the run from the government."

"They can call us whatever they want, but it won't change the fact that we're on the side of the angels more often than not."

Something inside her eased, and she brushed away a tear of relief before it had a chance to escape her eye. "You able to move over a little on that stretcher?"

He smiled and did. "With the right motivation, I can do anything."

She climbed in beside him, the metal *creaking* underneath them but holding, and closed her eyes as his arms wrapped around her. "Good to have you back. Don't ever do that again."

CHAPTER TWENTY-FOUR

Kevin stood as Richardson's assistant opened the door to the meeting room. "They're ready for you now." He exchanged a glance with his second-in-command, communicating his amusement at the oversight committee's belief that they somehow had actual power over him. Still, he didn't speak as he followed the suited man into the chamber.

They were gathered in a new location today, a conference room in the FBI's Washington headquarters. It was as plush and comfortable as any executive meeting space, with a credenza on the right wall supporting coffee carafes and various pastries, a high-tech monitor dominating the far wall, and vertical blinds that probably covered a long window along the left wall.

He walked to the beverage station and grabbed a heavy ceramic mug, filling it with coffee. He took his time about it, adding a sugar packet for the additional delay since he normally drank his coffee plain. Then he sauntered back to the table and chose the spot at the end nearest the door.

Tash had already claimed the chair in the corner that was positioned there for her. Several assistants sat in similar arrangements in the other corners.

Senator Richardson, who had taken over the chair position of the committee, began the meeting. "Mr. Serrano. Thank you for coming to meet with us."

He chuckled. "As always, please call me Kevin. It's not like I had much choice. I mean, oversight is in the name of the committee."

His joke fell flat, solidly setting the tone for what was to come. The representative from the CIA, a fifty-something man who was notably gaunt and wore round rimmed spectacles under an unruly shock of gray hair, replied, "The purpose of this meeting is to discuss your most recent operations. We'll start with the involvement of Senator Aaron Finley. What in the world made you think breaking into his home was an appropriate choice?"

So, we're playing hardball, are we? Problem is, none of you have ever seen how hard I can play when I need to. He nodded amiably, keeping his face and emotions locked down.

"First, allow me to remind you that Senator Finley received nothing more than scrapes and some bruises during the operation and is currently enjoying our hospitality at a fairly nice hotel. It's not as if we're talking lasting damage." He let a small smile appear at that statement, thinking that he'd like to offer an enduring wound or two to the folks in this room.

"Second, to your question, our mandate is clear. We are to capture or kill Sheen and her people before they can do something terrible with the artifacts they've collected and continue to collect.

"In service of that, sir, you can be positive no minor concerns like whether it's polite to break into a senator's home will influence my thinking. I have a job to do, and I will do that job as best I can. If the oversight committee wishes to start planning operations, I'm happy to step aside and let you do so."

It was an empty threat, and everyone in the room knew it. They wouldn't dare accept that responsibility, and he wouldn't give up his position without a fight if they tried.

Senator Borowski said, "Fine. Then explain how it came to be that the target of your operation, Bryant Bates, slipped through your fingers. Frankly, Kevin, the members of this committee can only conclude gross incompetence, based on what we know right now."

He paused before replying, meeting the eyes of the women from the FBI and Homeland Security, who were younger than the senators and the CIA representative, but no less fierce in their expressions of condemnation. "The situation has nuances you're not aware of, Senator, and I'm happy to share them with you. I would hasten to add that they're *not* things that fall under the committee's advance need to know.

"I didn't break procedure at any time during this operation. You wisely awarded me flexibility and doubtless knew when you did that I would exhaust every asset I have in service of my mission." He gave Borowski a hard look, and she nodded.

He continued, "The initial thing you need to be aware of is that capturing Bates wasn't an end in itself. While we hoped to get intelligence from him and did get a piece of information that was extraordinarily useful, that wasn't the only purpose of taking him."

The committee members' faces shifted from displeasure to interest. "We used him to set a multistage trap. The first was an ambush at the garage housing the vans that took part in the capture operation. We had no way to be certain Sheen's team didn't have some method of identifying and tracing them, so we decided to use that to our advantage."

He'd captured their interest and lessened the negativity they'd felt at the start of the meeting. "Sure enough, they hit that location a few hours after the operation. That they were able to do so revealed how effective Sheen's team is at gathering intelligence, which will be a consideration in everything we do from here on out."

Andrea Walsh from Homeland Security, a solid-looking blonde with long hair and a short temper, interrupted. "Do you know how they found the garage?"

From his side, Tash responded, "We're guessing traffic cameras. We don't have enough evidence to be positive."

Kevin nodded. "We learned more about how they fight during that battle. While they took no losses, we also emerged unscathed physically and in terms of intelligence. It was a dead-end for them, as we intended."

He paused, waiting for additional questions, but none came. "Then, as we were interrogating him, Bates had a medical crisis. Before he passed out completely, he surrendered the location of their new base. He didn't do it intentionally, of course. He was clearly out of his mind from the interactions of the truth serum we gave him and whatever drug he activated."

FBI representative Kiki Shelford was thin, with dark hair, dark eyes, and a dark attitude. She asked, "How did he manage to smuggle that in?"

"The cameras in the room show that he applied hard pressure to the area above his collarbone. Must've had something in there. We found his implanted locator but missed that one. In the future, we'll use MRI instead of x-rays. That's a lesson learned."

The woman nodded. "Understandable, and possibly a good idea to share across agencies."

"I would agree, but that's certainly your area, not mine. Anyway, we deployed the new experimental Army squads to guard Bates in case they made a play for him. They did and took at least injuries, and perhaps losses, during that fight.

"Perhaps more importantly, while they were busy doing that, we attacked their base. Those present were able to escape, which we expected. Not putting security around your operational center isn't the sort of mistake this crew would make. Now anti-magic emitters are deployed all through it so they won't be portaling back. They're without a home, and we'll likely find some useful intel as we process the place."

The people around the table looked impressed at that, another marked change from the beginning of the meeting.

"Finally, the battle gave us insight into how well our new Army allies perform in the field, which is to say, quite well."

Richardson frowned. "Who are these assets? Where specifically do they come from? How did you get access to them? Our understanding was that this was an idea only, that implementation would be much more long term."

"I'm not at liberty to share, I'm afraid. Still, they were ready, so we put them to use." Kevin spread his hands on the table. "So that's the past. Going forward, we'll have an eye on Finley in case some sense of loyalty sends them his way. It's doubtful, but it doesn't hurt us to keep a couple of people on him.

"Our main effort will be to pursue every hint of an artifact sighting in the hopes of finding Sheen and her team or blocking her access to them by taking the objects ourselves. At the same time, we'll deny them familiar ground to run to. When they do inevitably pop up their heads, we'll slice them off."

Questions and answers took most of an hour before he and Tash were able to escape. As they walked in the chill air, she said, "One of the soldiers might not make it. I received an update during the meeting. As near as we can figure, a ricochet, maybe even friendly fire, nailed him in an unlucky spot."

He shrugged. "That's the risk of playing the game. Sucks, though."

"If he does die, that's enough for a murder charge. Hell, we could probably make attempted murder stick right now."

"True."

She looked over at him. "Do we want to go loud with that? Blow it up in the media?"

Kevin considered that in silence for several seconds as they walked, automatically looking around him for any sign of danger or suspicious activity. *I need an outdoor vacation. Or, at least, a vacation from the oversight committee.*

"Not yet. We don't need to push any harder. If they're still worried about crossing that line, let's let them continue to worry rather than knocking them across it. Get max surveillance going again and wait for them to pop up. They're bloody and probably emotional, which could lead to a mistake."

Tash nodded and looked down at the ground as if she was still uncertain. Her voice was dark as she spoke. "Let's hope."

"You have doubts?"

She shook her head. "Not about our purpose. A little concerned that we've come out bloodier than them so far."

He nodded. "Time will tell. This is a marathon, not a sprint. Our resources are almost infinite, while theirs are dwindling by the second. Eventually, they'll run out of something—supplies, patience, people, whatever. Then we'll have them."

CHAPTER TWENTY-FIVE

Diana nodded at the techs as they entered the main room, completing her team. *Except for Tony, of course.* Ruby, Idryll, and Morrigan, who had been hanging out to offer whatever help they could, took that as a signal to leave. They shared their goodbyes and headed toward the portal chamber.

When only her people were around her, Diana said, "Thank you all for coming from such a far distance to join me." They laughed at the joke, despite how stupid it was. *The bunker is small. Get it?* She focused her will on remaining calm and confident, knowing they would look to her for leadership.

That thought drew her eyes again to Bryant. He was sitting in a stuffed chair in the corner, still hooked up to an IV but looking stronger than he had. She didn't like how long it was taking him to recover, but the healer had warned it might be a lengthy process. *He's safe. That's what matters.*

"Okay, first up, Tony is doing okay. He got hit in the legs, torso, and arm, so it will take a while for him to get back to us. The important thing is, he's safely in the hands of people who can help him.

"Deacon, Kayleigh, I want you to schedule drone flyovers of the clinic as often as possible without drawing suspicion. If you can figure out other surveillance, do it. Make sure you watch for computer break-ins, too. Serrano knows about our connection to Ruby, so everything that branches out from that needs to be watched."

The pair nodded, although she sensed Deacon's reluctance. It was no secret that he was irritated at the loss of his primary and secondary workstations. She imagined it would be like her losing Fury; the attachment was probably that strong. *He'll get through it.*

"I don't know how they found the island. I don't care. That's all in the past. They gave us a good punch in the mouth, and it's put us out of sorts for a bit. Now we need to focus on where we go from here. We'll start that by assessing our current situation.

"So, first, the negatives. Serrano's team is skilled, but not all elite if we include the ones in the garage. The people we faced off with during the op to rescue Bryant seemed military, to my eyes."

Cara spoke up. "Agreed. Some of their moves were familiar to me, so I'm guessing Army training."

Rath put on his best Bill Murray accent. "Army training, sir."

The room broke up, and Sloan replied in a better imitation, "That's a fact, Jack."

Diana grinned. "I guess *Stripes* is our next movie night selection. Getting back to business, we're in borrowed lodging again." She gestured at the bunker around them. "I know the time and effort we put into the Castle makes that all the worse, as does the loss of some personally valuable gear."

Rath said, "Practice knives. We should go get them."

Deacon complained, "Can't get my stuff back. Anik blew it up good, I'm sure."

The demolitions expert shrugged. "What can I say? I'm outstanding at what I do."

Diana interjected, "In any case, no, we're not going back there. They probably left a spot open for us to portal in, hoping we'd be stupid enough to go after our lost equipment. We're smarter than that."

She sighed. "I have to admit that I'm a little gun shy about putting down roots again. Too many losses, I guess. We'll keep our stuff mobile for now, live out of crates, not bother trying to customize any location too much. When we finish this meeting, whoever isn't assigned another task can bounce out and pick up some camping gear, so we'll at least have sleeping bags, cooking stoves, and those sorts of things."

Cara chuckled. "It'll be like basic training all over again."

Diana continued, "The last negative is the big one. I've thought about it a lot and have concluded that whatever shot we might've had at eventually getting the government to accept us back and clear our records is no longer viable. If it ever was."

Somber expressions greeted her words. Bryant replied, "I agree with Diana on this one. They've branded us as terrorists. I imagine some good people in the government might understand what we were doing and why we were doing it, but those aren't the ones in charge.

"My theory is that somewhere high up in this operation is a rotten apple, someone who's uninterested in anything other than seeing us gone. Could be they're planning to make a play to shutter all the ARES branches or integrate them with another agency. It wouldn't be the first time politics has reared its ugly head against us, although this is certainly the most vicious attempt."

Diana said, "We'll get to the implications of that in a moment. First, assets. Cara, what do we still have?"

"The gear we were wearing. The basic stuff we'd already packed out, some grenades, other consumables. We have enough anti-magic bullets to arm the team fully for the next op, but no promises after that. Some other odds and ends not worth mentioning."

Sloan shook his head. "That's downright dire."

Diana nodded. "It will present a challenge, to be sure. But we've faced lots of those, and we always come out on top."

Rath laughed. "It's always pretty hard on our buildings."

Cara joined the Bill Murray imitation fan club. "Blown up, sir."

Rath started giggling, then fell over on the couch, unable to control it. The rest of the team laughed at him, and Max joined in with a long string of barks.

When he finally wound down, Diana said, "Good to see we've all still got that positive spirit going on. Now it's time to talk about options. I want your input here because this affects all of us, more or less forever."

She paused while everyone collected themselves and focused on her. "We have several possibilities. First, we could go to ground here for a while. See what develops with the government while keeping our heads down and staying out of trouble."

Bryant growled, "That's what Serrano said he'd do if he were us."

Hank snorted. "As if we'd do anything that scumbag would. So that's a no. Next."

Diana nodded. She very much agreed. "We could relocate to Oriceran and keep our heads down there. We'd be roughing it a little, hunting for food probably, but it would be safer than being here."

Anik asked, "Are there any options that aren't hiding out and doing nothing?"

She shrugged. "We could focus entirely on trying to build lives as civilians, apart from each other, and get away from all this drama." She emphasized the last word, drawing it out.

Pride filled her as her team laughed, every one of them mocking that choice. Cara said, "We have a job to do. Those artifacts are still out there, and they're bad news. No one's better than us at dealing with them. That should be our main goal."

Everyone else agreed, and Diana nodded with a broad grin. "I'd hoped that's what you'd say, especially since it's the only one I thought through plans for." That generated another round of laughter.

"Okay, then. Kayleigh and Sloan, do what you can to

determine if any military branch has a program to train magicals. Start with the Army, since Cara thinks that's who we faced. We need to know if those people are active duty, contractors, or what."

Bryant added, "If they *are* active duty and under Serrano's control, that will tell us something important."

Kayleigh replied, "Will do. Deacon and I are going to need to buy replacement gear. Any problem with that?"

Diana shook her head. "Keep Cara apprised of spending since I'm now appointing her our honorary treasurer."

Cara groaned. "Isn't that a leader thing? What is it you do around here anyway, Boss?"

She ignored the comment. "Deacon, find us a warehouse. Everyone else uses them. We might as well, too. I'm sure Ruby won't mind if you ask Demetrius for some assistance in setting up the false paper trail. The faster the better, so if we can outsource part of it to someone trustworthy, that's useful. We need to rely on whatever help we can get at the moment. That's secondary to setting up surveillance to protect Tony, though."

He nodded. "On it, boss."

Diana drew a deep breath, then let it out. "I couldn't ask for a better team. Serrano thinks he has us on the ropes. We're going to show him that all we're doing is winding up for a power slam."

She slapped a hand on her leg to punctuate the thought. "Anyone who doesn't have a specific task, rest up for half a day. You'll handle getting our stuff moved into the warehouse once Deacon finds us one while everyone else takes a rest.

"Then, when night falls, we'll see what's happening in New Orleans. If that cult is still operating as Zeb thinks, we'll knock them down again, harder this time, and see if they have any desire to get up afterward and face us again."

CHAPTER TWENTY-SIX

Cara pushed another rolling crate from their emergency storage space through the portal into the warehouse Deacon had secured. She didn't know how he'd managed it so quickly, and a small part of her worried he might have sacrificed security for speed. *Nothing I can do about that right now, anyway. Just have to add surveillance and defensive gear to the list.*

She scowled and gave the stubborn case a hard shove to get it over one of the divots in the building's floor. The list of things they needed was getting pretty long, and the person power they had to create, buy, or install it wasn't nearly as extensive.

She released the crate to let it roll into position on its own while she walked up the metal stairs that led to the second-floor office Diana had claimed. Hank would be back soon with sleeping pads and bags for everyone. The arrangement suited Cara reasonably well. She'd never been one to care too much about fancy things, and like she'd said in the meeting, had roughed it fairly often during her military career.

She knocked on the door and entered, finding Diana leaning back in her chair, boots on the desk, and eyes closed. The other woman muttered, "What? Some of us are trying to sleep in here, you know."

Cara laughed and sat in the chair across the desk from the boss, putting her feet up. "You know, I remember when you hired me. Talking about all the great tech we would have, the cool digs we'd operate out of. I wanted to point out that events have proven you to be a lying liar."

Diana chuckled. "That's not true. We *had* those things. I checked those boxes."

"Breach of contract."

The other woman snorted. "Did you look at the papers you signed? I pretty much own you. Speaking of which, rub my feet."

Cara made a gagging sound. "One, no. Two, eww." They both laughed, and she continued, "Ultimately, we have good people, and that's what counts, I suppose. Who needs creature comforts like dependable heating?"

Diana nodded with her eyes still shut. "Exactly. That's the spirit."

Cara said, "I'm a little concerned about weapon supplies." With a sigh, Diana dropped her feet to the floor and opened her eyes. Cara sat forward, too. "I'm not sure what we need to do, but what we *are* doing isn't working all that well."

"I couldn't agree more. It's time we quit trying to protect those who are threatening us from the consequences of their choices."

"So, you're saying no more nonlethal?"

"I still like the idea of an initial barrage of nonlethal grenades when it makes sense. Good tactical choice. But yeah, time to kick up the effectiveness of our firepower."

Cara nodded. "Good. Okay. I think I can make that happen. Hank and I were chatting about it, and he has a source he trusts to be far more motivated by money than by any misguided sense of loyalty. To anyone or anything, as he put it."

The boss ran her hands through her hair, pulling it away from her face. "Don't forget, there's a reward out for us. By now it's probably more if we're turned in dead than alive."

"Believe me, that's a unique enough circumstance in my life that it never strays far from my mind. I get the sense his contact isn't particularly fond of any government."

Diana shrugged. "I trust you completely. Do what you need to do. Now get out of here and let me sleep."

As Cara stood and headed for the door, Diana resumed her earlier position. She chuckled. *Rest while you can. The worker bees have got this.*

<hr>

When Hank returned and Cara told him they had the go-ahead, he was more than willing to get moving on their weapons situation. They packed the guns they'd taken from the garage into a duffel that the big man threw over his shoulder. Then he opened a portal, and they stepped from the cold of winter to sunshine and warmth.

She asked, "Where are we?"

He grinned. "Mexico."

Cara turned her face up to the sun and closed her eyes in pleasure. "If we have to move again, I'm going to demand we go south. Enough with the cold and the snow."

Hank nodded. "I think the boss is a glutton for punishment."

"I'm sure excellent strategic reasons exist for us being where we are, probably having to do with Deacon and Internet connections or something." She dropped her head and shaded her eyes. "The world's gone mighty technological. I always thought I was savvy, but with every year that passes I seem to fall a little farther behind."

He clapped her on the shoulder. "Which is why we're the ones going after the weapons. Old-school people for old-school problem-solving."

Cara laughed, her mood lighter than it had been in some time. "True that. So, what is this place?"

Hank pointed at a building in the distance. They'd materialized in the middle of a large expanse of dirt with scrub grass and little else present. "Once upon a time, back when I was seriously committed to recreational fighting, this was one of the best places to do it."

Cara had accompanied him to a fight club and very much understood the appeal. Had things not gone as dramatically bad in Pittsburgh as they had, she probably would've regularly joined him for those activities.

"Anyway, the guy who owns it has his hand in a lot of pockets. Coyotes to move people across the border, some fencing of stolen goods, that sort of thing. No drugs, though."

"Good to know." Neither she nor Hank had any tolerance for people who would deal with illegal drugs. *Well, the recreational kind, anyway. Medical pharmaceuticals might be a different story.* The building grew and grew as they neared, turning out to be almost as large as the warehouse they'd rented, at least from the outside. "Damn. Big place."

"He has all his businesses in here. Bar in the front, arena in the middle, store in the back."

"The authorities don't bother him?"

He chuckled. "In this part of Mexico, police presence is thin. He pays a tithe to the force, as every business around does, and makes sure it's big enough that they don't feel the need to bite the hand that feeds them."

They entered the bar's front door. Only a few people sat at the square bar in the center, all of whom seemed very focused on their drinks. Empty tables populated the outsides, except for a small area with a couple of dart-boards. The floor was wood, the walls were old plaster, and the ceiling was open to show the rafters of the peaked roof.

Hank walked up to the bartender and exchanged a few words, too low for her to hear. Whatever it was, it caused the man's attitude to shift from professionally disinterested to respectful, and he nodded toward the back while reaching under the bar. Cara resisted warning Hank of the motion, figuring he'd seen it or knew it was coming. *Not my show, thankfully, because this is so not my element.*

They passed through a door marked "Employees Only" and entered a large space with a circle painted in the center. She scuffed her foot along the wooden floor. "Ouch. Do you get splinters when you go down?"

He nodded. "And in your feet, sometimes. I usually fight with foot wraps, but actual shoes aren't allowed, of course."

"Sounds like a good time."

He laughed at her sarcasm. "On many occasions, it was. I lost once or twice, and that was educational if not quite as entertaining."

They crossed through another doorway, this one requiring them to knock, be viewed through a sliding panel protected by a metal grate, and have the door unlocked for them. Hank strode forward and gave the person rising from behind a table scattered with papers a hug. "'Steban, long time no see."

The other man squeezed her partner, then took a step backward. He wore dark jeans and a black cowboy shirt with silver designs and buttons adorning it. Dusty harness boots completed the image. He replied, "You haven't been here in ages, *hermano*. You're one of my best earners."

Hank laughed. "Esteban here takes bets during the fights. Some of his people work the crowd now and again, tilting opinion one way or the other. Always to his benefit, of course."

The man in question grinned. "It's a living. So, what can I do for you? You here to sell? Too early in the day for a fight."

Hank hefted the duffel bag. "Trade-in and buy, more likely."

He looked over at Cara. Sharp eyes locked onto hers as he asked neutrally, "You vouch for her?"

"With my life."

Esteban's attitude switched back to full friendliness. "Well, all right then. Let's get you supplied."

He led them through another door into what had to be the rearmost part of the building. Weapons of various kinds were locked in cages around the room's perimeter, along with boxes and crates of military and military surplus equipment. He explained, "Sometimes people have a thing they don't need anymore. I take it off their hands and hold it until someone else needs it. I provide a service."

Hank laughed as he set the duffel down on a big metal table in the middle. "Check these out while we take a look." Cara followed him around the room, debating what they absolutely needed and what they only wanted, coming up with a larger than expected shopping list.

They returned to Esteban, who had spread the rifles out and summoned another man to check them over. He said, "Okay, what will you have?"

Hank replied, "Ten M4-slash-M203 combos, along with whatever grenades you've got to go with them. Care more about flash-bang, gas, and smoke than high explosive and projectile, but we'll want some of each. Add in bandoliers to hold the grenades."

Esteban nodded. "Easy. What else?"

"One of those crates of MREs, assuming they're still good."

"To be fair, they were *never* good, but they're not past their use date." He grinned as they laughed. "Is that all?"

Hank gestured. "I'll take that big Bowie knife you've got back there, as well."

The man shook his head. "You and the knives. I'll throw that in for free." They negotiated a sum that included the trade of the other weapons, and the man went off to collect their stuff.

Hank added, "Oh, and a bunch of ammo boxes for the rifles."

Esteban waved over his shoulder. "Already in the price. Knew you'd need them."

Hank thanked him, then said to her, "Lost my knife collection at the vimana. Had some good pieces there, too. World War Two stuff. Time to start rebuilding."

She laughed. "Sounds right to me."

A half-hour later, Esteban had crated up their purchases, and they were ready to portal it through to a portion of the warehouse that wouldn't indicate where it was. They'd had to trade most of their available cash since credit wasn't an option at this shop.

Esteban said, "You come back and fight soon, Hank. You too, *hermana*. No one will believe you can beat a big man, but I know you can since Hank told me so. So, I'll make tons of money from their small-minded prejudice." He grinned. "You'll get a cut and a percentage off your next purchase from me."

Cara laughed. "Consider that a date, then."

Esteban and Hank exchanged hugs. Then her roguish new acquaintance gave her one as well. "Stay safe, my friends."

Her partner replied, "Now that we have these, you can bet on it."

CHAPTER TWENTY-SEVEN

Diana lifted her sword in a salute, then stepped back into a defensive stance with the blade raised over her head and angled downward in front of her. Her left hand was extended with the palm forward, ready to block. She wore a tunic and a hakama, all white except for a scarlet sash at her waist.

Across from her, the sentience inside Fury wore his typical outfit, a black hakama under a scarlet top, with a faded black belt knotted around it.

He returned the salute, then slashed his sword in a vertical chop, generating a flash of light as if it had opened a rip that allowed the sun to shine through. When the stroke was complete, a Japanese demon had replaced him.

It wore a mask much like a kabuki mask but stylized and evil-looking, with horns and a red-painted frown. It wore the traditional leather armor of a swordsman in alternating black and red pieces. In its hands as it attacked with a shout were a katana and a wakizashi.

She ducked away from the first slash and brought her

sword across in a slice at his legs. He knocked it down with his smaller blade. Diana leaned back in the opposite direction and swiped her weapon up and around, catching his descending sword and redirecting it away from her. A snap kick connected with his stomach as he passed, but it didn't appear to affect him at all.

The demon screamed, a wicked sound made of scraping and pain, and charged at her again.

They continued their dance for a full minute. Diana focused on protecting herself while analyzing his attack pattern; a process Nylotte had drilled into her head over countless training sessions. Her mentor's ability to employ multiple fighting styles made her an amazing opponent to practice against and was probably all that allowed Diana to defend against the slashing blades currently seeking to end her.

Finally, she caught him repeating a pattern and stepped into his next swing rather than evading it. Her arm intercepted his so the sword couldn't reach her, and she stabbed her blade in through his ribs, then ripped it out sideways. When the stroke was complete, he exploded into sparkling glitter. It flew into the air, swirled for a moment, and coalesced several feet away into a new opponent, another Oni, this one bright blue with white horns and a scowl.

Her new adversary wielded a giant hammer, which was already hurtling down at her. *Can't block that. I'll break my wrists.* She dodged out of the way, and as the hammerhead hit the floor, he used the long handle as a fulcrum to jump across at her. His foot slammed into her chest.

She backpedaled and sliced with her sword, cutting off the tip of one of his boots and likely whatever had lain inside it. He hissed in anger and whipped the hammer around horizontally.

Diana leapt into the air to avoid it and smashed her feet down on the head as it passed beneath her. Her weight knocked the handle out of his hands, and she spun into a backhand slice, neatly separating his skull from his torso. Again, the defeated opponent transformed into glittering shards, and again it reformed into something new. Twin demons, this time, one black-skinned and one scarlet-skinned, each with grey features.

Their moves held an uncanny sort of symmetry, as if they were mirror images, as they circled her. She feinted at the one on her left and dashed toward the other, trying to get past him so she wouldn't have his companion at her back.

He clearly understood her intent and swung his swords into her path, forcing her to break off the charge. She exchanged a flurry of blows with him, metal ringing against metal. Neither of them gained an advantage.

Then his twin arrived, and its sword sliced along her side, parting her clothes and the flesh beneath. She cried out in a mixture of pain and anger and slashed wildly with her blade. It missed, but one of the enemies made the mistake of stepping forward into her range, thinking she had overcommitted. She spun, dropping beneath the pair of swords that went for her torso, and cut his legs out from underneath him. He exploded, but his twin stayed, and soon another demon had materialized.

As she backpedaled, her mind frantically sought solutions to being outnumbered. It found none. She fought defensively, trying to reserve her counterattacks until she could make a killing blow. She connected with a slash and sliced the arm off one of her opponents. Instead of the demon evaporating, only the detached limb did, and it came back as yet another enemy.

The new arrival was smaller than the others but wielded a wicked hook on a chain that it spun with a gleeful grin. Diana groaned at the unfairness of it all but launched herself into battle against the trio nonetheless. Three-on-one was too much, especially with the knowledge that anything other than a killing blow would make the odds worse. They defeated her quickly, two swords and a barbed hook plunging into her body simultaneously.

Without transition, she found herself kneeling across the table from Fury, both of them clad in formal robes. He was preparing tea, as he usually did when they met. The atmosphere was different than usual, not inside but instead outdoors in a well-tended gorgeous garden with cherry blossoms falling gently in the background. She bowed her head. "Beautiful."

He returned the gesture. "Thank you."

"Each of those demons was you, am I right? Not a construct? They didn't fight like mindless beings."

Fury smiled. "Indeed."

"I wasn't aware you could have multiple incarnations at one time."

He lifted a hand slowly so its trailing sleeve wouldn't bump anything and gestured to their surroundings. "In this place, my abilities are limited only by how much you interfere with my world." His smile and tone conveyed that he was teasing. "What lesson do you believe I was trying to teach you today?"

Diana was confident in her response. "That I can fight as hard as I like, give it everything I've got, but if I stay on the defensive, I'll eventually lose." She sighed. "I get it, but I couldn't find a way to gain momentum as each new problem arose."

He gave a single nod to acknowledge the correct answer. "It is a question of will, of mindset. Had you focused carefully enough, you would have been able to shift this realm we share. But you were pressed from all sides and thus too distracted to accomplish that."

She nodded slowly, understanding that he was talking about the world outside as much as this one. "That situation isn't going to change, is it?"

He shook his head. "You would know better than I, but my opinion is that it will not." A low chime sounded in the distance. "Now your attention is needed elsewhere. I look forward to seeing you again."

Diana opened her eyes at Cara's knock on the door, then rose to her feet and unlocked it. Her second-in-command entered, wearing a slightly concerned expression. "Should I ask why you're in here alone with a naked blade, or should I assume everything's okay?"

She laughed. "Communing with Fury."

The other woman nodded. "I'm almost afraid to see Angel and Demon again. They're going to be ticked that I haven't used them."

Diana sat on the edge of her desk. "We've been busy while you were gone, slacker. Completely unpacked. Ruby's people helped. We'll have a splice for water and power by tomorrow, so I can send Sloan out to do something else rather than using his magic to keep the place bright enough to work in."

Cara nodded and clasped her hands behind her back. "What, if I may be so bold to ask, is the plan?"

"First, how did your shopping trip go?"

Cara grinned. "Hank's friend is quite a character. But we returned with M4-slash-M203s and a bunch of grenades for them. They won't take our shock or web grenades, unfortunately."

Diana shrugged. "We can repurpose those rounds into handheld stuff or have someone carry a launcher in addition to the rifle. Hank's big. He can handle it."

Cara chuckled. "Definitely. We also grabbed some odds and ends, some MREs, that sort of thing."

"It's a start, which leads to the answer to your question. We have two primary goals. One is to improve our situation however we can. Surroundings, supplies, whatever."

"And the other?"

Diana grinned. "Kick some artifact-loving-religious-zealot ass and do our best to keep those evil items out of anyone's hands but ours."

Cara clapped once. "I'm so very in."

CHAPTER TWENTY-EIGHT

Rath leapt with a shout, drew a throwing knife from his vest with his right hand, and hurled it through the air at his target. It tumbled twice and its point stabbed into the large "X" drawn on a sheet of paper taped to a wooden crate. He landed cleanly, spun, and backhanded another blade, this time with his left. It pierced the paper and wood directly beside the first.

He didn't like the warehouse's practice facilities as much as he'd liked the Castle, and neither of them could compare to the vimana, which had been the best training space *ever*. Still, the warehouse had come with some debris, empty crates that had never gotten moved out, and Anik had helped him move them into place to use as training dummies. Max ran beside him as the troll charged into the empty area that separated them from the targets.

He threw two more blades, then dispatched another pair in a single throw, emptying his vest. Max barked, and Rath nodded. "Six throws, six hits. Not bad."

He pulled the knives out of the crate and checked each

blade before slipping it back into its vest sheath. Regret over losing his practice knives crossed his mind, but Diana was right. It was far too risky to go back and get them.

Rath reran the course, this time adding acrobatic moves —throwing his blades after coming out of a somersault, in the middle of a cartwheel, or while sliding. Max barked and dashed in circles around him, forcing the troll to concentrate on the dog's position as well to avoid hitting him. *Which is good training. Smart partner.*

As he slid the last blade back into his vest, a footstep sounded behind him. He turned to find that one of the Mist Elves who'd been assisting in readying the warehouse had approached. He grinned at her. "Hi."

She smiled. "Hello to you, friend. I'm Shinsha. You're very good with those knives." She was beautiful in the way that many elves were, sort of ethereally so, and her long hair was pulled back at the sides to display her pointed ears.

"Practice, practice, practice. Although not a very challenging setup."

"Would you be willing to show me how to do it?"

He nodded enthusiastically. "Of course." He loved training and teaching equally, which was to say, a lot. He showed the woman how to hold the knife, how to throw it by the handle or the tip, and how to flick her wrist to get it to tumble properly.

Of her first six throws, only one struck a target and stuck. By the end of a half-dozen rounds, all of her attempts stuck, and most hit the paper if not the "X" in the middle.

She seemed pleased with her success and thanked him. He replied, "Any time."

Her expression turned thoughtful. "If you're willing to let me try something, I might be able to make your training a little more interesting."

She called to a nearby Mist Elf, a male, and asked him to set up a force shield to protect the knife-throwing area from the rest of the warehouse. Then she moved into the back corner, well out of the way of his throws, and gestured.

A flicker of movement in his eye peripheral vision caused him to turn back toward the targets. Six enemies had appeared. They shimmered and were faintly translucent. He immediately understood that they were an illusion, something Mist Elves were, as a rule, particularly good at. He grinned. "Better targets."

She nodded. "Don't let them touch you." They lurched into motion, and he grabbed his knives, racing to the right to put some of them in the way of others. His first knife flew true and struck the nearest, then paused in midair before gently settling to the floor. *Magic is awesome.*

He raced around, throwing the rest of his blades at the moving targets. He'd missed only one of them by the time he was out of projectiles, but Max dashed up to that one and dove through it while snarling and biting. Rath clapped and yelled, "Awesome!"

Shinsha laughed and motioned for the other Mist Elf to come over to her while Rath collected his knives. When he was ready again, she said, "This time they'll fire magical bolts at you. There will be more, enough for Max, too. My friend Mitrian will handle the force shield and catch your knives."

Rath nodded at the man. "Thank you."

He laughed. "No problem. I hope you'll teach me some knives when you finish."

"Will." Then the troll launched himself into motion again. The nearest enemy raised a hand and sent a blast of light at him. He jumped and spun along his long axis in mid-air, almost as if rolling on the ground, and came out of it throwing as soon as his feet touched. The blade passed through the figure without a problem.

This time, he faced twelve figures instead of six. Bolts of light shot in at him, and he was forced on the defensive, jumping, spinning, and twisting to avoid them. Max dashed in and took one out, biting him in the leg and whipping his head around as if he would throw the figure. He wondered if the dog saw them as real or understood they were illusions. *Probably knows. Maxie is smart.*

Rath found an opening to hurl a knife and took out an enemy. He whipped another blade, catching one that had been about to blast Max, and the dog eliminated one with a snarl. The troll lost himself in the battle, diving, flipping, and rolling, and retrieving one of his already thrown knives to toss it again. By the time all twelve were down, he was tired, and Max was panting.

He walked over to the Mist Elves. The woman looked like she'd put in some effort, too, and was grateful for a reprieve. He said to Mitrian, "Now?"

The man laughed. "Definitely. Let me get someone else over here to watch the shield."

In that fashion, Rath taught most of the Mist Elves in

the warehouse the basics of knife throwing. In the process, he learned their names and a thing or two about them. When he'd run out of time and needed to rest a little before whatever the night would bring, he offered to teach any of them whenever they wanted. They accepted his offer and gave him high fives, fist bumps, or in the case of Shinsha, a kneeling hug.

As he walked toward the office where his sleeping bag awaited, a feeling of connection and community warmed him from inside. *This is why we need the Network. So someday all magicals can feel this connection if they want to.*

As he climbed the stairs, he tumbled over names in his mind. *Community net? No, too long. Love net?* He laughed. *Probably give people the wrong idea. Troll net? Hmm. That one's got potential.*

CHAPTER TWENTY-NINE

They'd set aside a corner of the warehouse on the same side as the office for their arming space. There were no lockers or benches or other comforts, only crates and boxes, kind of like a band used while on tour.

Diana finished buttoning the uniform top over her base layer, pulled the connectors for the shock gloves free, and adjusted the shirt so it felt right. She strapped on her belt next. It held all the suppression grenades she'd been able to fit on it.

She was still willing to preserve the lives of their opponents as long as it didn't risk her team and had embraced the idea that an initial barrage of grenades might be an effective choice. It would likely be especially useful against non-magicals who couldn't redirect the munitions with a wave.

Her vest went on next, and she slipped the bandolier holding the grenades for the under-rifle launcher over her shoulder. She gave those around her subtle looks as she secured it to the belt at her hip.

The team seemed different. Harder, maybe. *More focused, definitely.* She wasn't sure if the new weapons caused it but felt that was probably a contributing factor. For a while, they'd tried to be something they weren't, forced by circumstances into an uncomfortable situation. *Circumstances, and my decision.* She shook her head. *Might've been a mistake, but at least none of my people died for it.*

She slipped grenades into the bandolier, most of them nonlethal. Fury went on next, and she checked her pistol and rifle to ensure they were fully loaded. Extra magazines slid into the slots on her vest, and she grimaced at the fact that she only had one backup full of anti-magic rounds for each weapon.

Cara must've been reading her mind. "We're going to have to rob a bank or something, Boss."

Diana shook her head. "If we're lucky, the cult will be hoarding gold bars we can steal."

Hank growled, "Gambling is the answer. Maybe Deacon could hack a casino."

It wasn't far from the truth. Certainly, the infomancer could keep breaking into government systems and getting them access to money that way. But that was a risk already and would become more of one once the federal agencies they targeted figured out what her team was up to. *We'll jump over that bridge when we come to it.*

She holstered her pistol and attached the rifle to its strap, then rose and checked her people. They all had full armament, except for being as low on additional anti-magic rounds as she was. Hank had agreed to lug along a drum-fed grenade launcher in addition to his other gear, which would doubtless come in handy.

Bryant would be spending the op at the base, listening in and providing advice if needed, but nothing more. She stepped up beside him and murmured, "Any sign of trouble here, you portal out. Don't be a hero."

He nodded. "Not my scene. That's more a *you* thing."

"Good. Remember that." She turned to the rest and increased her volume. "Come on, lazy people. Quit dragging your feet. It's time to move."

Fifteen minutes later, they stepped through the rift into the basement of the Drunken Dragons tavern in New Orleans. Zeb was waiting for them, ready to provide a portal to the location where the cult was operating. Kayleigh and Deacon ran up the stairs with heavy bags on their shoulders, headed for a nearby hotel that boasted the best Internet connection in the area. Sloan and Anik each carried a crate with a drone inside that they'd deploy when they got close.

The dwarf opened a portal that showed the roof of a building. "Rath, this one's for you." The troll gave him a high five as he ran through. Then Zeb summoned another, which revealed a wooded area on the opposite side. He apologized, "It's not that close, but this is the only cover around there. Believe me, I looked."

Diana nodded. "We can use a veil to get in. No worries. Thanks, Zeb."

"Thank *you*. I don't want to see any more of my people disappearing."

"Nor do we. Into the breach, folks."

It was a night with clouds covering the moon. Their glasses rendered their surroundings as if it wasn't yet twilight, providing a good view of the five-story office building. The schematics they'd found had indicated the possibility of a basement, as well.

Now that she was present in person, Diana was as annoyed as she'd been when she'd initially seen it on paper. She muttered, "If we go in on the first floor, they can get us from below and above. So, since we're not especially skilled at digging, I guess it's time to fly."

Rath stood on top of the same hotel Deacon and Kayleigh had rented a room in. He was waiting for the "go" signal and fidgeting with the small box he held. It appeared as if the cult building wasn't active on any computer network, so the infomancer had no way of judging what the security inside might include. While the drones they'd brought would be able to supply some information, he'd asked Rath to install a network enhancer on the roof.

Rath had agreed immediately. Any excuse to fly was worth it. He also had a long, thin cable attached to a grappling hook wrapped around him. It was incredibly strong for its weight and would be enough to allow any team member to climb the side of the building if necessary.

After five minutes of looking down at the city, which was still hopping at two in the morning, Deacon announced, "Okay. I'm online. Kayleigh will be ready in a second. Permission to launch Troll Flight One?"

Diana laughed. "Troll Flight One, cleared for takeoff."

Rath grinned. "Awesome." He ran to the edge and leapt into the air, instructing his AI to provide his navigation overlays. The office park was a little over a mile away. That required him to stay on the currents that would keep him aloft, except for brief moments where he might have to dip to transition from one to the next.

He banked and flew, taking far fewer chances than usual due to the extra weight he carried. He lost altitude faster than expected, but fortunately, he'd started more than fifty stories up. The drones were active by the time he neared the building, and their feeds appeared in the corner of his goggles, letting him know a little more about his target.

Gwen provided a giant red "X" layered on the roof as his destination, along with an arcing flight line to reach it. He followed her instructions and touched down within a foot of where the lines crossed. His wings snapped back into their container, and he ran to put the enhancer in place and turn it on. Deacon said, "Signal's good. I'm connected. Still no access to anything in the building."

Diana asked, "That's strange, right?"

"Yes. Suggests they don't have any security, alarms, that sort of thing. Which, you know, would be a little weird for an illegal enterprise."

Hank replied, "We don't know that they're technically illegal."

Cara countered, "We saw the ones in New York try to kill someone."

"Yeah, but that was them, not these people. They could be a kinder, gentler set of fanatics."

Diana pointed out, "They tried to kill us, remember. That's something."

The big man chuckled. "I'm not sure those skeletons were life-threatening but sure."

Rath ran to the side and attached the grappling hook, then let the line fall to the ground. Deacon announced, "Activating jamming anyway." Both drones sped above the building and hovered. Diana and Cara flew up to the roof to join him by magic while Hank climbed.

After he arrived, Cara teased, "We could've carried you, Hercules."

He growled, "Not the way you fly." The others laughed.

Diana said, "Okay, the plan hasn't changed. We four go in. Face and Khan, you're our backup. Be ready to blast in on the first floor if we need you. Deke and Glam, keep an eye out with the drones and give us whatever support you can. Plus, monitor the local PD. We don't want to get caught here."

Rath added, "Or anywhere."

"I stand corrected. Or anywhere. Game faces on. Let's go."

CHAPTER THIRTY

Diana led the way to the small building that enclosed the stairs leading down. The door was unlocked, as was the one at the bottom. Cara opened it enough to stick the fiber-optic camera from her sleeve through. The view showed a standard office setup with an open central area and offices all around. Heat signatures were present in three of them, horizontal and mostly motionless.

Diana said, "Probably sleeping. We'll position by the doors, enter at the same time, and hit them with the stun gloves. Then we'll tie them up and take whatever seems useful. Rath, you'll stay in the center, ready to help." No one registered a complaint, so she ordered, "Go."

They moved into the main area, then each headed to their door. A moment later, three people dressed in the familiar cultist robes were unconscious. Diana's search revealed nothing worth taking, and the others reported the same. Rath, who had drawn his batons, pointed with one toward the far end. "That looks like the only stairwell, next to the elevators."

"Okay, let's do it." They repeated the process with the camera to enter the stairs. Halfway down, Diana froze and pointed. "Tripwire." She looked down over the railing to find it was attached to a bunch of tin cans, which would *clang* together if the line moved. "Are you freaking kidding me?"

Rath replied, "Real do-it-yourself feel here."

Hank observed, "It's amateur hour again."

The troll laughed. "This building needs a better class of criminals."

Cara groaned. "Okay, Joker. It could be a decoy, with more advanced stuff around. But I sure don't see it here."

They all stepped over the line, then descended even more cautiously, watching for improvised alarms and traps as well as the more traditional types. They reached the door to the floor below without additional incident but found this one locked. Diana commented, "Weirder and weirder."

Cara nodded and pressed her electronic lock pick against the panel beside the doorway. The latch released, and she slid the door slightly open with one hand while pocketing the device with the other. She used the camera again, and what showed up was entirely unexpected.

This brightly lit room was full of people. Six of them wore cultist robes and seemed to be overseeing twelve men and women wearing only their underclothes and surgical masks. On the table in front of them rested a variety of powders and liquids. Diana murmured, "Drugs? Really?"

Cara corrected, "Magical drugs." Diana looked closer and spotted what she'd seen. When the work finished at one table, they moved the products to another, where one of the people in the robes cast an incantation over it. It seemed quite involved and also incorporated spraying the powder with something. From there, it went to a third spot where they put the black substance into tiny plastic bags.

Hank observed, "Well, that's alarming. Artifacts *and* drugs?"

Cara replied, "They don't scruple about human sacrifice, so this isn't a stretch."

Diana ordered, "Magical shields. We don't want to breathe that stuff in."

Her second-in-command warned, "That'll crack our crystals."

"I know. Nothing for it. Let's not wind up in the hospital because we inhaled whatever that nasty stuff is. So, here's what we'll do."

When she finished explaining the plan, Hank took a moment to reorder the canisters in his launcher's drum. Cara opened the door far enough for him to launch six gas grenades into the room. The robed people in the rooms scattered after the first landed, but the vapor was quick-acting, and they collapsed in rapid succession.

One of the cultists managed to throw a fireball in their direction, which caught a nearby crate on fire, but Diana coated it with ice before it could create any real havoc. Shock grenades knocked out the masked workers.

She ordered, "Get a sample of that stuff. Actually, grab a bunch of them. We'll send it around to make sure everyone knows what's going on."

Rath replied, "I've got it." The rest of them applied zip ties to the fallen, ensuring they wouldn't escape when they woke up. The cultists again had nothing useful with them except a couple of wands.

Diana gave them to Rath so he could add them to his collection. "Think we set off any alarms?"

Cara and Hank shrugged. Deacon replied, "Still not sensing anything, for whatever that's worth."

Kayleigh reported, "Jamming remains active, so they won't be able to signal out."

Diana shook her head. "I feel as if there's some vital piece of understanding about these people we're missing. I don't know what it is. It vexes me. Anyway, let's head down another level."

They returned to the stairwell and started down. Rath asked, "Go straight to the basement, maybe?"

"I'd like to, buddy, but we can't risk leaving scumbags on an upper level to come down on us from behind. We need to make a clean sweep."

"Thought I'd ask."

She smiled down at him. "You always should. You're one of the smart ones. Not like Croft."

The camera revealed only a wide-open space on the third floor. It was similar to the fifth level but without the limited furniture that rested in the center up there. They cautiously crept through the door with weapons facing in all directions.

The carpet looked hard-used, scuffed, torn, and stained. No lights were on, unlike the fully lit fourth floor and the fifth, which had emergency lighting. Diana conjured a ball of fire wrapped in a force sphere and sent it up to hover, then guided it around the room so they could get a look at everything.

Cara said, "Training space, maybe? Those stains could be blood."

Hank nodded. "That was my thought too."

When the globe had completed its circuit of the room, finding nothing but closed doors leading to offices, Diana replied, "As good a guess as any. We need to check the offices to be sure they don't hold any surprises."

Hank replied, "I'll do it. Croft, cover me." They moved together to the first office on the left. He turned the handle and threw the door open. "Nothing." The pair shifted to the next, but before he could open it, a stream of gunfire pierced the door, bullets smashing into his vest and knocking him backward.

Diana reflexively called up a force shield in front of him, which thankfully stopped the rounds. Hank rose and winced. "That sucked. What do we have?"

The room that had been empty of heat signatures now showed a vertical cylinder glowing along its length. She replied, "Looks like a military bot." The door fell away, shredded by the continuing fire, and confirmed their attacker was a military attack robot. "Where the hell did they get that?"

Cara shook her head. "Stole it, maybe? Or a knockoff from another country? I can't imagine they have any relationship with our military."

"Agreed. Put that on our list of things to investigate. I'll drop the shield. You hit it with an EMP."

"I'm keeping track of our list of things to buy. Someone else can remember what we need to investigate. Also, ready."

Diana stopped blocking the way, and the bot rolled

toward the doorway. Cara threw the EMP, which latched onto the robot magnetically and detonated. With a sizzle, the machine went dark. Diana said, "Well, that was bizarre. Fortunately, not too difficult."

She realized that she'd once again unintentionally tempted fate when the gunfire erupted from the other three sides of the room.

CHAPTER THIRTY-ONE

Diana reacted as she had before, throwing up three walls of force in the path of the incoming bullets. A few rounds made it through before the barriers fully formed, and she took a hit in the vest. *Thank goodness they're programmed to aim for center mass.* "Little help."

They each carried an EMP disc, and Diana tossed hers to Cara as the other woman flashed by. Her second found an angle toward the one opposite the stairs and flipped the disc. The bot let out a complaining whine as it went down. Hank took out another with his. Rath circled behind a fallen one to get a firing line and dispatched his with a throw that looked a lot like the kind he used with his knives.

She snapped, "Check the other doors. Shields everywhere until we've cleared them." She focused her mind and created a force shield in front of half the remaining doorways in the room. Hank and Cara did the same with the others. Rath stepped to her side and observed, "Again, totally weird. Why?"

Diana nodded. "Defensive measures, I guess. I suppose they could be for training. But those were real bullets that shredded the doors."

Hank reported, "Clear," as he checked out one office, then moved to the next.

Rath shrugged. "Was loud. Maybe half defense, half alarm."

She replied, "Could be." She added another force shield, this one covering the stairwell while her team cleared the room, then let it fall when they finished. "Let's get a move on, people."

They moved carefully to the second level, where the stairs unexpectedly ended. It looked like it should go on, but a concrete wall stopped further progress. Diana's scanner indicated it was several feet thick, meaning they couldn't blast through it, even if the staircase did continue downward on the other side. *We could break through the floor, but that doesn't seem smart, either. Noisy and time-consuming.*

Opening the unlocked door revealed another empty area much like the one above but without as much damage to the rug. It had full lighting and seemed welcoming. Cara said, "I don't like the look of this."

"Agreed. Forcing us into this specific location screams trap." Her glasses flicked through their detection modes, and when they reached infrared, a maze of lines appeared in her visual field. "Well, there you go."

Hank said, "That's insane." It looked as if someone who wasn't quite right in the head had designed it. The infrared beams crossed the space wildly, all of them at different angles and seemingly random inclinations.

Diana replied, "Not how I would've done it, that's for sure. I don't see an obvious kill switch anywhere, do you?" The others responded in the negative, and she sighed. "Well, there's nothing for it but to pass through. Unless we want to head home, which is seeming more and more attractive by the minute."

Rath said, "Let me check out the other side."

She frowned. While it was true that his acrobatic skills probably made him the best choice, many kinds of traps would still be dangerous to him. "What about motion sensors? Pressure plates? We should blast our way through."

He shrugged. "Sometimes it's good to be tiny."

She shook her head. "No. If we hadn't knocked out a bunch of robots upstairs, I'd be willing to give it a try. But they already know we're here if they're listening. So, there's no point in trying to be quiet anymore."

They swapped to standard rounds and shot out most of the electric eyes from the doorway. Defensive systems engaged in response. Gas canisters deployed and several fragmentation grenades rolled out into the room. They closed the door and stayed protected in the hallway while the defenses did their thing. Diana cleared the remaining vapors with a wave of force magic, confining it in one corner, and they made their way down to the first floor after switching magazines again.

There, they found an utterly normal-looking reception area. Cara said, "Well, that's unexpected."

Diana had to agree. The cult was apparently putting forth an illusion of normalcy, at least in the place where they first met visitors. It was all whites and pale pastels, a blend of comfortable and high-tech.

They moved through the space carefully, swiveling weapons to cover all the angles, but found no enemies. Rath said, "Brochures," and Diana turned to look where he stood. Sure enough, a set of shelves beside him held a bunch of pamphlets.

She grabbed a sample of each kind, figuring they might be useful later, and shoved them into a pocket. "So, on the one hand, murderous cult. On the other, all the trappings of a quasi-religion."

Hank said, "Want to be the next Scientology, maybe."

Cara let out a small snort. "Gotta start with celebrities for that kind of success."

Diana shook her head. "This could be the scariest thing we've seen from them. It suggests a bigger plan in operation and might work to recruit some people into joining up."

Rath's voice was uncommonly dark as he added, "Or maybe that's how they get sacrifices."

She nodded. "Could be. Although you'd think there'd be an evidence trail showing people came here before going missing."

Cara replied, "Someone would have to care, and organizations like these prey on those without connections. And in New Orleans, the police are probably pretty busy to begin with."

"Well, the upstairs was weird, but this floor's downright creepy. Let's keep moving." The staircase to the underground portion of the building was far less clean and polished. It showed signs of age and a lack of maintenance.

Everything felt a little wet, chilly, and decidedly ominous. It ended at a thick, heavy door with several sliding bolts to lock it.

Cara frowned. "Odd to have locks to keep things from below from coming up."

Rath suggested, "Monsters."

Diana growled, "That pretty well describes the whole organization, I think. But you're right. It's beyond weird. Hank, spike the door so it can't close behind us."

"You got it, boss." Each of them carried wedges they could use to block doors open or closed as one of the useful odds and ends in their equipment belt. Diana grabbed the door handle, drew a deep breath, and yanked it open. Their displays had shown no signs of heat or life in the next room, suggesting it was empty. The glow of light from the stairway into the dark space proved that conclusion to be incorrect.

The spill showed enemies nearby, and her glasses shifted into lowlight mode to electronically illuminate the rest. Arranged seemingly randomly around the area were a bunch of skeletons—too many to count—presumably similar to the mechanical kind they'd faced before. Unlike the ones embedded in the walls, these looked less polished, with sharper edges along their bones. Red lights came to life in their deep eye sockets.

Diana ordered, "Take them down." She didn't want to waste anti-magic bullets on robots and taking the time to change mags would likely get her in trouble. She thrust her left hand forward, expelling a force blast to knock several away from her.

Fury was in her hand a moment later, and she slashed

down through the neck and shoulder of the nearest in a continuation of the draw. The skeleton's body kept advancing even with the head detached. Diana kicked it in the ribs, then whipped Fury through to separate its spine. She knocked over the legs, which continued to try to move, then targeted the next.

Her team had launched into action only a half-second behind her. Hank was delivering punches to the nearest that crackled with shock detonations. Cara had drawn Angel and Demon and was a spinning blur off to her left. When she did get a brief flash of the other woman's face, a wicked smile covered it. *I'm not the only one who needs to let off some steam.*

Rath focused mainly on smashing his baton into the sea of skeletal legs and had already dropped several enemies to the floor. Rather than finishing off their crawling forms, he simply kept moving through the press, bringing any that came near him down to his level.

Diana misjudged a block and took a hard punch to the shoulder that sent her stumbling backward a few steps. "Ow. These things hit like trucks."

Hank replied, "Well then, let's wreck 'em." He was almost a berserker in the way he embraced hand-to-hand combat, and she supposed that if she possessed his magical power, she would be the same. *Feeling the magic build up inside and releasing it at will would make fighting a distinct pleasure, above and beyond the satisfaction of measuring oneself against an opponent.*

Since she couldn't do that, she contented herself with chopping up the ones Rath had dropped to the floor and taking out any others who came across her path. It took several minutes to finish the automatons, but they were never in much danger from them. Hank had taken a deep cut from one of his foes and paused to quaff the contents of a healing flask to deal with it. Cara had sheathed her knives and was kicking through the debris, looking for anything useful they could take with them, probably.

Rath reported, "Found the door." It, too, had bolts to secure it, so what was below couldn't climb up.

Diana chuckled. "Maybe we should lock them away and let whoever it is starve down there."

Spooky, echoing laughter resonated through the chamber. She remembered it and the voice that followed from the last time they'd tangled with the cult in New Orleans. "Surely you want to know what's at the end of the yellow brick road, don't you, dearest? Do come downstairs and join us."

Diana sighed and muttered, "Drama queen." She turned to her team, who had gathered behind her. "It might be best if I went alone to check it out. She seems to have a problem with me."

Hank shook his head. "Nope."

Rath added, "No way, no how."

Cara rolled her eyes. "Shut up and move, Boss."

CHAPTER THIRTY-TWO

The stairs wound down and to the side, then opened into an entirely unexpected chamber. Another set of steps continued down from their entry point to a floor about six feet below. It reminded her of a church sanctuary, likely because of how the ceiling rose a story and a half above to a peak and how it naturally drew the eye to what would be an altar in a traditional religious building.

Here, it was a wide platform with a throne resting on it. Between Diana's team and the woman seated in that over-sized chair stood a collection of people in robes, organized into two symmetrical lines on either side of the walkway leading forward through the space. Flickering illumination came from torches on the walls and suspended candelabras throughout the room. The chamber had a distinctly medieval vibe.

Cara muttered, "It's like the place in New York."

Diana replied, "It is. Although at least there's no flaming brazier for human sacrifices here."

Hank said, "Yeah, but they've got those," and gestured to the side.

She hadn't noticed the four symmetrically placed transparent rectangles since her eyes had been focused on the woman in the front instead. Inside each was a naked figure, their wrists attached by chains to the top of their cage. Two men and two women stood imprisoned there, all appearing to be college age or just beyond, and each had the heavy-lidded look of sedation. *Or maybe some kind of magical drug, given what we saw upstairs.*

She turned her attention back to the regal figure at the far end of the room. As before, Maîtresse Mambo Severine Eschete's attire looked like funeral garb. Her crown of tentacles was in place, although this chair was far less ornate than the last one they'd seen her in. The dark makeup shrouding her eyes and lips was as dramatic as Diana remembered, as was the snake wrapped around her neck.

Her long ebony braids looked like they had bones threaded into them. On either side of the chair were the large black dogs that had accompanied her at their last meeting. A new addition was a pair of figures who stood behind the canines, a woman and a man.

From this angle, they appeared to be twins, the light to Eschete's dark, white-haired, white-skinned, and adorned with colorful tattoos that covered their bodies. They wore hardly any clothing, only enough leather to keep things PG-rated.

She magnified her display to get a better look and saw the same sort of crazy in their eyes that she remembered in their leader's. The woman on the throne called, "Please, approach."

Diana kept her hands on her rifle but angled the barrel toward the floor to still the urge to pull the trigger as she paced up the middle. The others followed, and she was confident they would've arranged themselves to keep an eye on all directions.

It was at moments like this where having a team that simply knew what to do was most valuable. *That's why we train.* A smile twitched the corner of her mouth as she imagined Rath echoing those words, then she refocused on the wild-eyed fivesome in front of her.

Hank said, "I've got the right side."

Cara replied, "Left."

Rath added, "The dogs are mine."

Diana gave a slight nod but didn't reply. When they were three-quarters of the way toward the throne, she stopped walking. "You need to let those people go, right the hell now."

Eschete laughed, and her mad cackle echoed from the surrounding surfaces. The cultists remained silent. "They are here of their free will."

"They're drugged. Consent isn't possible in that state."

The cult leader shrugged. "They chose their path when they refused my invitation to join us voluntarily. Now, I make you the same offer. Join, and we'll skip the ordinary preliminaries. Within the hour, I could grace each of you with Rhazdon's blessing." Shadow tentacles emerged from both of her arms and reached out to gently pet the dogs beside her.

The sight made Diana's stomach turn. *She's got two. No*

wonder she's insane. She swallowed against the discomfort rising from her belly. "They're here, now?"

"Of course. We have enough for anyone who would wish to join us."

Cara whispered, "That has to be a lie."

Hank muttered, "I don't think these red robes have them. Or at least not all of them do."

Diana replied, "How about we take the artifacts and go, along with the four people in the cages. Then, you all stop doing what you're doing, and we'll call it even." She wouldn't give up on taking the cult leaders down, but if a way existed to get the captives to safety, she needed to try it at least.

The other woman laughed, as did the twins at her sides. "Impossible. Besides, the artifacts belong to us. *All* artifacts do. Soon, they will return to my hands."

Diana couldn't hold back a snort of derision. "Who do you think you are, Rhazdon returned?"

Eschete leaned back in her chair with a wide smile. "Of course not. I am The Severine, Goddess of Shadow."

Rath muttered, "Like Norman said, 'We all go a little crazy sometimes.'"

Diana said, "Well, your highness or whatever, we're not going to join your little bunch of, uh, whatever you are. So, release your prisoners and hand over the artifacts, or things are going to get messy."

The Mambo shook her head. "You've made your choice. It's unfortunate. You in particular would have made a good servant." With no change in her tone or routine inflection, she ordered, "Kill them."

Diana yanked up her rifle and sent a burst of anti-magic bullets at the throne, traversing the barrel to make sure she included the dogs and the twins beside her in the barrage. As at their last meeting, physical barriers shot up to protect the woman, this time a metal container that surrounded those on the platform. The sound of a top latching into place defeated her next notion of launching grenades into it from above. She muttered, "Damn it to hell," and turned her attention to the nearest transparent cube.

She sent a blast of force magic at it, intending to break the confinement and follow up with a more focused attack on the cuffs holding the captives in place. Instead, her power struck a shadow shield that formed over it. A sinking feeling of horror flowed through her at the sight of the woman writhing inside that translucent purple barrier. The female prisoner was whipping her head back and forth, clearly screaming. A demon's face tattoo had appeared on her chest, looking bloody and raw.

Diana said, furious at her inability to stop it, "The bitch just infected the front right captive with an artifact."

CHAPTER THIRTY-THREE

Cara replied, "Same front left." She pulled her trigger and sent bullets into the nearest cultists, who had surged toward her. Magical shields appeared but didn't stop her barrage. Several dropped, and the rest scattered, circling to take her from the sides.

She grabbed a grenade from her bandolier, rammed it into the breech of the M203, and pulled the trigger. The gas grenade went off in a cluster of red robes, and they fell. She belatedly warned, "Gas," and used a wave of magic to push it away from her.

She loaded and fired several more grenades, exhausting her supply of the gas option and taking out many of the cultists. Then things were too close for ranged combat. She let the rifle hang and set herself to take on the man coming at her with a long knife in his hand.

Cara waited until he committed to a strike, then crossed her arms in an "X" block, stopping the blade as it stabbed down at her. A subtle twist of her wrists later, she had his arm gripped in her hands.

She curled her fingertips into the nerve that ran along his forearm, and the blade dropped from numb fingers. Without releasing him, she lifted her foot and slammed a front kick into his ribs, breaking them. That boot was only on the ground for a second before she kicked his feet out from underneath him, sending him hard to the floor, where at least one more bone cracked from the impact. She muttered, "Moron," drew Angel and Demon, and searched for someone else to fight.

Hank already had a gas grenade loaded in his rifle, so it took him less time to fire all of his than it had Cara to get hers out. He smiled as the sound of her launcher continued after he was done and looked forward to teasing her about it later. Their ongoing competition for enemies defeated was one of his favorite things.

Delivering punishment to people who sorely deserved it was another. He waded into the nearest, punching, blocking, and kicking, taking them out of the fight one after the next while building up his magic reservoir. Some threw magic at him, but he dodged it or endured it, depending on his level of success.

His objective was the woman in the transparent cage ahead of him. She'd stopped writhing and rose to stand in the center. She thrust out her arm, tentacles smashed the cube open, and the shadow barrier dissipated. He reported, "One artifact is active. Moving in."

He raised his rifle, trained it on her, and pulled the trigger, sending three anti-magic rounds at the woman. Her tentacles reached out and grabbed nearby figures, lifting them and shoving them in the way of the bullets as she jumped down from the platform. They then threw the damaged bodies at him, forcing him to dodge aside. "Shit. She's using the cultists as shields and projectiles. That's hard-core cold."

Diana said, "Don't hold back. If they're infected, we can't help them. They need to go down."

Hank saw only two options. One, get in close and hope that he could overpower the magical tentacles with his magic. Or find a way to hit her from a distance. He opted for the latter, knowing that more artifact wielders might be entering the combat at any moment if they weren't involved already.

He grabbed a high-explosive grenade and launched it at the woman's feet. It detonated and sent her flying backward, protected in a cocoon of shadow, and killed the cultists nearest her. He'd immediately loaded another of the munitions and pulled the trigger. It slammed right next to her, blasting the stone into rubble that flew upward and cascaded down.

While she was dazed, he emptied the rest of his rifle into her body. The anti-magic bullets passed through her purple protection without hindrance. The artifact clawed its way free of her lifeless form, and he slapped a force box around it to trap it so it couldn't infect anyone else. He said, "One down," and hit the lever to release the empty magazine from his M4.

As Diana attacked the woman in charge, Rath had raced forward, stabbing, hacking, and slashing with his batons. One was torn from his hand by an overzealous block. He stabbed the lucky cultist who'd separated him from it in the throat with his remaining baton as a reward. The stun blast dropped him instantly. After a few more moments, his weapon no longer sparked, its power depleted. He grabbed and threw grenades from his belt—shock, flash-bang, and web, locking down or disabling the cultists around him.

The sound of breaking glass caught his attention an instant before shadow tentacles reached out and seized him from the nearest transparent cube. The man had bared his teeth in a grimace of something between anger and pain. The tentacles pulled Rath toward him as if the man was going to bite him. The troll chuckled inwardly. *Talk about biting off more than you can chew.*

He called upon his innate magic and grew, reaching eight feet by the time he reached the six-foot man. He'd been husbanding his strength against that moment and thrust both his fists forward, no longer resisting the arms trying to crush him but using the momentum their push gave him to strike his foe in the chest.

His opponent coughed blood as something inside him broke, but the tentacles didn't release Rath. *That's fine. Close enough.* The troll slammed his head forward, his forehead crashing in against the man's skull. His strong hide and currently massive bone structure won out easily, and his enemy collapsed. The artifact didn't separate from him, which meant he wasn't dead and could get back into the fight.

Rath punched him a couple of times with the shock gloves that had stretched and now only covered his knuckles, then turned to a pair of cultists who had attempted to close from nearby. He spread his arms wide and roared at them. Wisely, they ran for the exit, and he looked for more red robes to harass.

Cara rushed at the infected man nearest her. He had leapt down from his perch and summoned a shadow sword in each hand. The artifact had attached itself to his shoulder, and tentacles grew out of it. They swayed in an almost hypnotic pattern, clearly ready to join him in his attack. She said, "This one seems to have good control. Looks like a successful joining."

He strode forward to meet her rush, slashing swords in descending diagonals as the tendrils reached for her head. Cara spun to her left, avoiding one sword, and brought Angel around in her right hand to block the blow from the other. A tendril got close to her, and she stabbed it with Demon.

The man shrieked as her artifact blade severed the tip of the grasping shadow limb. It didn't instantly regrow, contrary to those of other artifact wielders they'd faced in the past, and Cara filed that away for later consideration.

Then his swords came at her again, this time stabbing straight ahead. She blocked both down with inside-out circles of her daggers and kicked forward into the space she'd opened. The tentacles blasted down and grabbed her foot, and she emitted an embarrassing yelp of surprise.

She pushed off with her other foot, hurled herself at the man, and shoved her blades at the tentacles, forcing them to release her or get sliced through. Her weight met his, and he stumbled backward but didn't go down.

She fell and landed on her back, aware that it was a terrible position to be in. She hurled Angel at her foe, knowing the dagger would take her to task for doing so later. He contemptuously knocked it aside with his sword and arrogantly smiled down at her. She drew her pistol and put three rounds into that grin.

The man fell. The artifact broke free and ran at her, and she yelped again as she locked it down with force walls on four sides and the top. She retrieved her dagger and readied herself for her next foe.

Diana fired a full magazine of anti-magic rounds at the artifact wielder in front of her, but the other woman used her tentacles to grab nearby objects and interpose them into the stream. It wouldn't have been her choice to expend her anti-magic ammunition on unconscious cultists, but she couldn't do much about it. With their enemies mostly taken out by the gas grenades or used as shields, it was more or less her against her opponent, one-on-one.

She drew Fury with her right hand, grabbed a stun disc from her belt, and hurled it at the artifact wielder. A tentacle slapped it back toward her, and Diana waved it away to detonate against the container protecting the throne. She tried another grenade, this time web, and it met the same response.

Okay then, let's do this. She summoned a shield on her arm and muttered the incantation to activate the full body shield charm in her bracelet. Shadow tentacles attacked, and she intercepted some with the arm shield and others with Fury's keen edge. The ones that managed to evade both those defenses failed to penetrate her other shield.

The protection from the charm wouldn't last all that long, so Diana knew she had to finish the combat as quickly as possible. She ran forward, a reckless move that resulted in a shadow tentacle's sharp barb sneaking through and scratching her face as the charm's defense wilted. The point almost caught her eye as it scraped past. Still, the rush got her close, and she slashed through all the tentacles near their source in the woman's chest.

She punched in with the shield, but her foe raised her arms and took the blow on them, protecting her face. Fortunately for Diana, and unfortunately for her enemy, it looked as if the other woman had been a captive for a while. She seemed weak and slightly emaciated, both of which made her less effective in a fight lacking the shadow tentacles.

Diana slammed her knee up into the woman's stomach, and she crumpled. The former agent followed up with a punch to the face with the shock glove, knocking her out.

Unfortunately, it didn't take her out of the fight. As Diana summoned force magic to bind her foe's feet, the tentacles boiled out again. She stepped back and angled her sword to intercept them, but she wasn't their target. The tentacles grabbed their host's head and wrenched it to the side, breaking her neck and killing her. Then the artifact jumped free and scrambled toward a cultist. Diana, shocked and more than a little horrified, locked it down with force magic.

Laughter echoed through the chamber. "Such prowess. You will make an excellent addition to my collection when the time comes."

The metal protection around the throne fell away to reveal a shimmer as Eschete—*no, wait, The Severine*—her dogs, and her scantily clad underlings vanished a second before Rath's thrown dagger would've embedded itself in the leader's throat. At the same instant, the three artifacts also disappeared from their cages.

Diana shook her head. "Make sure that fourth one is locked down. How the hell did she do that?"

Cara suggested, "Maybe she's attuned to the artifacts somehow?"

"I kind of hate these people."

Rath nodded. "Me too. Definitely bad guys and girls."

Hank said, "It was a good throw, Rambo. On the upside, we captured an artifact. On the downside, it's still in that dude."

Diana sighed. "We need to portal him away. Send him to the Paranormal Defense Agency. They'll know what to do. Hercules, you take care of that." He nodded and moved off to that task.

"Croft, let's see if any of these folks are still alive and get them out. Then we'll do the same for those we left bound upstairs. Khan, Face, we have to make sure no one ever finds this place. Rig the tunnels down here to explode. As a bonus, she won't be able to use it again."

The men replied, "Acknowledged."

Kayleigh's voice came over their comm. "Who the hell *are* these people, anyway?"

Diana shook her head. "I don't know. But I guarantee you we're going to make it our business to find out."

CHAPTER THIRTY-FOUR

Diana and her team were seated on collapsible camp chairs in the warehouse, forming a circle in the middle of the training space. She said, "So if we believe the crazy lady's words, the cult is gathering artifacts. Which isn't good."

Sloan observed, "That's *our* job."

Cara laughed. "Right? Exactly what I've been saying. Next thing you know, the government will hire them to replace us."

"The leader lady had two," Rath contributed.

Diana nodded. "I noticed that as well, buddy. Pretty rare for artifacts to coexist in the same person. Maybe that's why they're gathering them, trying to find combinations that will work together?"

"They're making the artifact version of super soldiers. In a lot of ways, it would be to their benefit to infect more people with one than for a few to have multiples," Hank pointed out.

Kayleigh shrugged. "Seems like our mission is

unchanged, then. Get the artifacts and keep them out of the hands of those who would misuse them. Now we're not getting paid to do it."

The group nodded, and Diana said, "Agreed. To accomplish that, we need to continue to gather more and better equipment and actively search out artifacts. We'll start that part by checking out the place in Pittsburgh that Rath's Network friends mentioned."

Bryant, who looked stronger but still not completely recovered, spoke up. "I've been thinking about it, and I can't get past the idea that someone in the government is using us as a cover for something else. It's time to see if I can figure out what's going on there."

Diana replied, "As soon as you heal."

"Sure."

She wasn't fooled and snapped, "Bryant."

He laughed. "Honest. I won't push it."

"That'll be a first."

Kayleigh smirked. "Peas in a pod, you two."

They finished discussing the details of their next moves, then broke up to rest. She drew Deacon aside from the others. "Did you handle that thing I asked for?"

He nodded. "Sure did."

Diana grinned. "No time like the present."

***

Kevin Serrano had arrived at his office to start his day earlier than his usual six am. He was surprised to find Tash there, and they chatted as they each made coffee in the small kitchen. He asked, "Know anything more about New

Orleans?" Their freelance watchers there had reported an explosion. The local news media had picked it up shortly after, something about an office park.

She nodded. "Yeah. I woke up our other people in town to see what they knew. They'd heard rumors a cult of some kind was operating out of there."

"Artifact cult?"

"They didn't have any more info. They're folks we're paying for information, so frankly we were pretty lucky to get what we got."

He chuckled. "Fair enough. Let's move some reliable people down there to investigate."

Their conversation was interrupted by Cassandra, the lead tech, who looked like something had unexpectedly woken her up. She confirmed it when she said, "I got called in. There's something you should see."

They followed her to the control center, where she waved over one of her subordinates. "Tell them what you told me."

The man nodded. "A video went up on YouTube a little while ago tagged with your name as metadata." He tilted his head toward Kevin. "Our servers isolated it and pulled it down before anyone could see it. Well, we're pretty sure of that. Can't guarantee it."

Kevin replied, "Understood."

"Anyway, we've run it through our detection systems, and it's clean. We haven't watched it yet."

He took a long drink of his coffee. "Let's see it, then."

An image appeared on the big monitor, showing a woman dressed in jeans, a t-shirt, and a leather jacket. Behind her was a blank and uninteresting metal wall.

Tash stated the obvious. "It's Sheen."

"It is. Play it."

Sheen came to life. "This is a message for Kevin Serrano and Natasha Kline. Here's the deal. We're done trying to play by your rules. Collectively, my team and I resign from our former positions.

"You, your people, and the government have nothing to fear from us. That is, assuming you decide to leave us alone. We'll let bygones be. But know that every action taken against us from this point forward will meet with an exponentially harsher response."

She walked toward the camera, growing bigger in the image, seeming to lock eyes with them across time and space. "This is your only warning. The gloves are off. Quit hunting us, and all will be well." A small sneer lifted her upper lip. "Choose differently, and things will be worse. *Much* worse." She gave the peace sign, and the image froze.

Tash said, "Well, that was decisive. Shall we close up shop, boss?"

Serrano would've liked to make light of the situation, as his second-in-command had done, but recognized the look in Sheen's eyes. They'd pushed her as far as she was willing to go and reached the proverbial line in the sand. *Unfortunately, my job doesn't allow me to stop.*

"Bring everyone in. We'll need more of everything. More personnel, more gear, and more allies. We can't let up, which means she's not going to, either."

Thank you for reading the third book in this new series, and for continuing on to read these author notes!

So, in the ongoing "Hey, that was a shock to me, too," I didn't anticipate the team losing the base under Bannerman's Castle. I put a lot of research into that. I had *plans*. But as Heath Ledger's Joker says in The Dark Knight, "I try to show the schemers how pathetic their attempts to control things really are." Mine clearly was in that case!

Book four in a series is always a pivot point, at least the way I write them. Things can be expected to change, but hopefully do so in unanticipated ways. I've got some interesting things cooking, and look forward to finding out which of those ideas make it to the page!

Life is a bit of a grind right now. October and November are always like that for me, as are February and March. I'm not sure why, but I've learned to recognize the signs. I'm truly grateful to have the opportunity to write my way through the doldrums – it's both hobby and job, pleasure and vocation.

I've started playing *Mass Effect*, a decade after most finished it. I remember trying it out, way back when, but failing to get hooked. So far, I'm *interested*, but not quite engaged. Hoping to become so, though. I've heard that Shepard's story is great, so I'm willing to give it some time to grow on me.

With *What if...?* completed, we've moved on to a rewatch of *Justified*. This is probably the fourth or fifth time we've watched the completed series again, so we're doing it in the "Cut out the boring stuff" format. See a character we're not fond of? Fast forward. Episode we remember hating? Skip it. It allows us to really revel in the writing and the stuff we love. Probably the show's creators would hate that, but it is what it is.

Watched *Black Widow* now that it's on Disney+. I enjoyed it. I get the criticism of the superhero films as being too cookie-cutter, but then again, we're on Fast and Furious TEN, so that seems a little like an overly-focused anti-Marvel critique to me. Sure, there are things that could be eliminated from the film, but I feel that way about most movies. But overall, a perfectly cromulent experience.

In the land of audiobooks, I've finished *Ready Player Two*. It wasn't as good as *Ready Player One*, but was better than I remember. And Wil Wheaton is great. Now I'm either going to go into Scalzi's The Collapsing Empire trilogy, which I loved, or Elvira's memoir. I've been a fan of the Mistress of the Dark for a long time, and I'm sure the story of her life is fantastic. Plus, she narrates it, so that's an extra treat, to be sure.

I'm having a hard time reconciling the fact that the

actor who plays Paul Atredies in the new *Dune* is also going to be playing *Willy Wonka*. Like... you're messing with my ability to love the sci-fi here, people.

I'm almost ashamed to say that I'm reading the *Foreigner* series for the third time in a row, although I did read *Ready Player Two* and the newest *Black Jewels* novel in there, too. Something about the world CJ Cherryh has created calms me. I think it's probably the elegant ritual of that society's interactions, as well as the comfort and caring between the main character and his bodyguards. The first book is a little hard to get caught up in, because there's a historical piece that sets the stage and isn't representative of the rest of the book or series. Still good, mind you, but not as captivating.

Anyway, enough babble from me. I'll see you on the other side of Book 4!

Reminder again - If you're not part of the Oriceran Fans Facebook group, join! There's a pizza giveaway every month, and Martha and (usually) I and all sort of fun author folks show up via Zoom to chat with our readers. It's a great time, and the community feel to it is truly fantastic. Oriceran Fans. Facebook. Your phone is probably within reach. Do it!

Before I go, once again, if this series is your first taste of my Urban Fantasy, look for "Magic Ops." I promise you'll enjoy it, and you'll get more of Diana, Rath, and company. You might also enjoy my science fiction work. All my writing is filled with action, snark, and villains who think they're heroes. Drop by www.trcameron.com and take a look!

Until next time, Joys upon joys to you and yours – so may it be.

PS: If you'd like to chat with me, here's the place. I check in daily or more: https://www.facebook.com/AuthorTRCameron. Often I put up interesting and/or silly content there, as well. For more info on my books, and to join my reader's group, please visit www.trcameron.com.

Okay, so the first text that came through with, "Thank you so much for the postcard! My granddaughter will love it," I thought – they sent it to the wrong person. And I was so busy I didn't even get time to reply.

That was last week, and I was in Vegas at the author conference and…

Then there was the email from an old friend that said, 'thank you for the birthday card. See you next year.' You're welcome?

By the fourth message that said it was so nice to get a postcard rather than just bills the slightest inkling of a memory came back. Oh yeah, I think I mailed out a bunch of postcards I picked up at Graceland when I was touring with Craig Martelle.

If you've been following the saga, you're probably already suspecting that chemo brain was at work – and it was. It's nice to know that even in the middle of the haze I'm out there spreading the love.

And I took some delight from my reaction that

everyone else was getting it wrong – not me. Good self-esteem even when befuddled.

Plus, I was out there spreading a little goodwill and didn't even remember. There has to be some extra karma points in that somewhere.

I'm at the part of chemo where it's ended, and the chemicals are slowly leaving. Kind of like they came in, peeling back a bit at a time. Every day it's getting a little easier to look in the rearview mirror and maybe see a little more clearly what just happened all year long. There are a lot of really good life changes I got out of it – more on that in future author notes – but one small one that I plan to keep is that when faced with a mind that wandered, I went with it.

I recognized that fighting was futile and letting go of worry or micro-managing might even be like a vacay. I recognized that part of the serenity prayer that talks about the wisdom to know the difference between what can be changed and what just is happening.

It meant that I did have to ask people to repeat their question a lot more and let them feel about that however they needed to – and I found out how loving and caring the people around me are. Another bonus. I let others carry more of the weight for a while and things kept rolling forward. Those are great things to discover. That I'm a part of something wonderful but not the driver of it. A definition of a healthy community and involves so much less stress. More adventures to follow.

CONNECT WITH THE AUTHORS

TR Cameron Social

Website: www.trcameron.com

Facebook: https://www.
facebook.com/AuthorTRCameron

Martha Carr Social

Website: http://www.marthacarr.com

Facebook: https://www.facebook.com/
groups/MarthaCarrFans/

Michael Anderle Social

Website: http://lmbpn.com

Email List: http://lmbpn.com/email/

https://www.facebook.com/LMBPNPublishing

https://twitter.com/MichaelAnderle

https://www.instagram.com/lmbpn_publishing/

https://www.bookbub.com/authors/michael-anderle

www.ingramcontent.com/pod-product-compliance
Lightning Source LLC
Chambersburg PA
CBHW050251110726

47898CB00007B/2366